Tejas Desai was born, raised and live [...] as a Supervising Librarian for Qu[...] Wesleyan University and holds a MFA in Creative Writing and Literary Translation from CUNY-Queens College. He is the author of the international crime series The Brotherhood Chronicle and The Human Tragedy literary series. In 2012, he founded the New Wei literary movement which seeks to promote provocative and meaningful narrative artists. His articles on literature have been published in *The Huffington Post* and other publications.

Copyeditor Christine Keleny is an award-winning author, reader, editor, book designer and publisher. She loves writing and helping others publish the book of their dreams through her publishing company: CKBooks Publishing. You can find all of her books at christinekelenybooks.com.

Praise for *The Brotherhood*

"A powerhouse of a novel that has well-drawn, engaging characters and a fast-paced plot that will keep you guessing. Well-crafted dialogue adds to the depth of the book, which is deeply rooted in religion and politics. With no clear line between the "good guys" and the "bad guys," *The Brotherhood* explores its deeply flawed but very interesting characters, and Tejas Desai leaves you wanting to read more about them. Thankfully it's part one of a series."—Vijay R. Nathan, Author of *Escape from Samsara: Poems*

"Everything and everyone and anything aren't what they seem, and even as you adjust your logic to keep up *The Brotherhood* keeps you guessing all the way ...The best way to describe *The Brotherhood* is simply this: a Mickey Spillane novel with a Bombay (or is it Mumbai...bloody hell) flavour...set in New York City. Betrayal, religious hypocrisy, greed, and sexual nastiness...it is nice warm cuddly pulp fiction with a nice global marinade."—The Evil Parrot Book Club

i

Other Books Released by The New Wei

The Brotherhood Chronicle

The Brotherhood by Tejas Desai (2012)

The Human Tragedy

Good Americans by Tejas Desai (2013)

Independent Books and Blogs Recommended by The New Wei

A Brie Grows in Brooklyn by Brienne Walsh (an online blog found at http://abriegrowsinbrooklyn.com)

Waiting for the Bomb by Richard Livsey (2013)

The Other Son by Allan Avidano (2014)

The Depression of The Blue Rainbow Sprinkle by Kacper Jarecki (2014)

Escape from Samsara: Poems by Vijay R. Nathan (2016)

THE BROTHERHOOD

*

THE BROTHERHOOD CHRONICLE
VOLUME 1

*

Tejas Desai

*

Second Edition

With a Note from the Copyeditor by Christine Keleny

ηƱ
THE ΠEƱ ƱEI

New York

The Brotherhood by Tejas Desai

Second edition published by The New Wei LLC in Fresh Meadows, New York, September 2018

ISBN Number: 978-0-9883519-7-4

Library of Congress Control Number: 2018910241

Table of Contents

DEDICATION

To Seshaaunti

For giving me

The Portable Faulkner

INTRODUCTORY QUOTE

"On seeing you, with your form touching the sky, flaming in many colors, with mouths wide open, with large fiery eyes, I am terrified at heart, and I find neither courage, nor peace, O Vishnu!" Arjuna to Krishna in the *Bhagavad Gita*

PREFACE BY THE AUTHOR

I return to my first published novel with tremendous excitement and some regret. I am proud of *The Brotherhood*, and its sequels, *The Run and Hide* and *The Dance Towards Death*, are even better. But this could have been a much different book—and most likely would have never been released to the public—if not for the revolution of self-publishing.

Let me give you some history. In the summer of 2000, between my freshman and sophomore years at Wesleyan University, I completed a short story collection called *The Brotherhood* about a diverse group of Indian-Americans centered around a Hindu religious organization. The title was inspired by the communist organization in one of my favorite novels, *Invisible Man* by Ralph Ellison. After some criticism from a professor regarding its lack of dramatic tension, I shelved it and tried other projects. For years, I struggled to find my voice and learn my craft, working on novels, stories, screenplays, and stage plays. All the time, I was trying to get an agent and get published, but despite much success in high school and college, I couldn't get anywhere in the real publishing world.

While obtaining my MFA in Creative Writing at Queens College from 2007-2009, I rewrote *The Brotherhood* featuring a similar Hindu religious organization but with completely different characters and a crime plot. I submitted the first part of a multi-part novel as my thesis, but even then, I was unhappy with it. At the time I was constantly rewriting my works, changing plots, characters, storylines, and experimenting with many different narrative styles.

During the next two or three years, the novel was completely rewritten over twenty times. At one point, the book was 500 pages long. Ultimately, I settled on a 300-page version, about 85,000 words, which is what agents and publishers said they wanted in a novel. And then I started to shop it, sending it out and going to conferences. I got initial interest from several agents, but the book was rejected for various reasons, sometimes without a reason, and sometimes I didn't even bother submitting it based on contradictory advice. In the meantime, I was also getting my stories rejected from literary journals, even as I was getting notes back telling me how great they were, something I already knew.

In January 2012, I took a trip to India as research for Volume 2. During the trip, my uncle took me to a fortune teller. He looked at my palm and told me I would be published in six months. I thought this was ridiculous. Since I had worked for a literary agent for several years, I knew that even in the ideal scenario, an agent would take at least a few months to read a manuscript, and in the unlikely case the agent decided to sign a writer, then the agent would have to send out proposals. If it sold, once a contract was signed, the hardcover wouldn't come out for another year. That would mean at least a year and a half, in the best possible case. But as it happens, a confluence of events made the fortune teller somewhat correct.

First, in the early spring, I met a small publisher through a friend. This publisher told me he liked the book but that I would have to tighten it up. I was given a deadline of six weeks, at which time the book would be reevaluated. So I started to rewrite it, but I also became paranoid. This publisher didn't use consignment with bookstores, didn't pay advances, and simply sold copies to small bookstores, which might result in earning $10,000, or so I was told. Of course, if they couldn't sell it, it wouldn't be published. It sounded like a plausible scenario, but nevertheless, not one that I'd ever been taught was legitimate when I worked in the publishing industry. But I was excited to rewrite the book into a tighter, more commercial entity (this is what I had been told by some agents too: tight writing sells!). So I went ahead with the rewrite despite expressing my reservations to the publisher.

Around the same time, I had met an agent at a book talk. I sent him the manuscript and asked him for advice on the publisher. The agent rejected the manuscript—he said it "wasn't for him"—but advised me against the publisher, saying he probably wasn't legitimate, and told me instead to self-publish on Amazon.

Nearly finished with the rewrite, I began to argue with the publisher, and ultimately decided to break from him. I sent the rewritten, more commercial version of the manuscript to the agent, telling him I was sending it to others, too. He responded immediately with interest and read it within one day. When I called him, he told me that while no publisher would take it, he could help me self-publish it through a new noir crime novelist company he was forming. He would place a trailer in the back of another client's book, I would write a sequel that we would also self-publish, and then he would try to pitch the third one to major publishers.

I was very excited to finally have an agent and consented. He sent me his contract. I immediately sensed a problem since the contract featured strange clauses which benefited him and a clause at the end which would necessitate me paying back an advance if the book wasn't delivered. Maybe I shouldn't have evaluated agency and publishing contracts for years. I marked up nearly every clause, correcting it based on my experience of how it should be, and sent it back. Of course, he immediately rejected me.

For once, rejection didn't make me feel dejected. Instead, I felt free. I knew what I was born to do. I would create my own company and publish the book myself. This is when The New Wei, my literary movement promoting meaningful, provocative narrative artists, was inseminated. For years I had been disappointed by contemporary "literary" fiction published by major and independent publishers, forcing me to read classic books that were more interesting in content and well-crafted in effect and meaning. Balzac, Faulkner, and Dostoyevsky were my favorite classic authors, yet no one in the contemporary literary sphere seemed to match up to their unique ability to create worlds that mirrored and critiqued their own societies in entertaining yet thought-provoking ways. It was rare that I would read a literary book that would have interesting, complex characters and compelling storylines that didn't involve bland, upper middle-class worlds. Most literary authors of my generation were hipsters writing cute books. Only noir fiction truly critiqued and explored society, yet most of the best noir fiction was written in the 1950s, and even the contemporary masters like Elmore Leonard and Richard Price were either deceased or of a much older generation. Much modern noir was also formulaic or overly wrought. And while I had commercialized my book, I had also made it more readable, tightening up the themes while quickening the pace.

I was fed up with the emptiness of contemporary literature and the fickleness of the publishing industry. So, I embraced the power of self-publishing and created a movement that would promote and encourage provocative works. But when I looked up self-publishing, I realized I couldn't just put it up on Amazon and expect people to be interested. I needed to do some kind of pre-level marketing. With some experience in making small independent films, I decided, why not make a trailer? I wrote a script, sent out ads in Craigslist for actors, and did auditions in my basement. I enlisted friends to help me, and they recommended me to my cover designer and cinematographer. I had plans for a more provocative trailer featuring the character of Lauren, but the actress never showed up for her audition. So, I pared it down. We were able to film the trailer in a single day, and later, my friend, Kacper Jarecki, and I edited the green screen backgrounds with footage that I had shot separately. I purchased the rights to two musical scores, and we added it.

I have to admit the final product of the film trailer wasn't perfect. Many of the scenes ended up being awkward, and the backgrounds were clearly edited in. That said, I thought the trailer did work in terms of pacing, and the music was good. I put it out into the world nevertheless and hoped people wouldn't assume the quality of the book would be commensurate with quality of the trailer.

I got somewhere around thirty sales on the first day I published the book online. A couple of months later, I got more than 250 downloads when I gave it away for free on Amazon. The book never became a bestseller, but it did put me on the map. I was also able to learn what worked and what didn't as I went along. I tried nearly every strategy for promotion, from readings to book fairs to ads to fliers, and I believe I've learned my lessons for the release of this second edition and the two sequels.

What did readers think? Most readers generally thought it highly readable (I got messages from readers who absolutely loved it) and a great jumping off point for a more complex series. And that's what it is. A page-turning, thought-provoking mystery thriller which not only stands alone but also leads into a more expansive literary universe.

This second edition is meant to expand the understanding of The

Brotherhood Chronicle's literary universe for those who have read it and to heighten the reading experience of new readers. Understandably, some readers may be confused or put off by the Hindu and Indian terms, another reason why many agents wouldn't touch it. But this is a way the book stands out from others of its ilk. It challenges the reader to understand and immerse themselves in a different world, and the two sequels, which delve into Thai, Australian, and Islamic cultural terms and slang, do the same. The expanded Glossary of Hindu Terms should be very helpful, but so should the map of New York City, the list of characters, and the study guide. The trivia questions are fun and could lead the reader to sources outside the book. The text has been freshly copyedited and proofread, but don't worry, if you purchased the first edition, the story hasn't changed; the characters, chapters, and timeline are no different. Some of the language and spellings are altered, that is all.

For those who are new to this book, enjoy its mystery and thrill, and prepare yourself for the no holds barred collision course of the unexpected that is this series. The first book is set in New York City and its immediate environs, but the next two have multiple locations and settings: Thailand, India, and North Carolina. The series is a richly detailed multicultural and multinational stew of our times, but a continuous and turbulent thriller all the same.

Tejas Desai
September 2018

NOTE FROM THE COPYEDITOR

It was a pleasure working with Tejas for his sixth anniversary reissue of *The Brotherhood*. It is an intriguing mystery that is a multicultural immersion into New York City and its suburbs by an author that knows of what he speaks. The main character, Niral, is an American-born Indian who is trying to find his way and to balance the life his immigrant parents want for him within Indian culture and the sometimes gritty existence of life in one of America's largest cities. Not everyone makes it, and when a good family friend is found dead, he is pulled into the mystery by his family and circumstance, forever changed by what he finds.

Christine Keleny, CKBooks Publishing Editor

MAP OF QUEENS AND ITS IMMEDIATE ENVIRONS

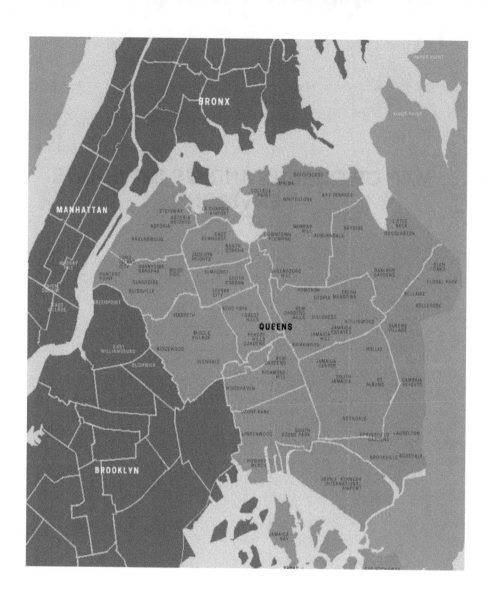

LIST OF MAJOR CHARACTERS

(AND SOME MINOR ONES)

Niral Solanke—a failed writer working for a private investigator, Stan Lorenzo

Prakash Solanke—Niral's father, a retired police officer

Heena Solanke—Niral's mother

Priya Mehta—a promising graduate student at NYU whose mysterious death starts the novel

Amrat Mehta—a Harvard dropout who has dedicated his life to his version of Hinduism

Dilip Mehta—Amrat's father, an accountant

Kirti Mehta—Amrat's mother, who passed away many years ago

Vishal Patel—a wealthy hedge fund manager and a graduate of Yale University in Connecticut

Meetal Patel—Vishal's sister, a journalism graduate student in Chicago

Narendra Patel— Vishal's father and the head of The Brotherhood's North American chapter

Kaunti Patel— Vishal's mother

Stan Lorenzo—Niral's boss and Prakash Solanke's former partner in the NYPD

Detective Denny Savard—NYPD detective investigating Priya Mehta's death

Lance Portman—custodian at the church building

Lauren Juvonich-Adams—Vishal's friend from Yale, a visual artist

Roberto Tragliani—the manager of The Dock

Bhen—founder and spiritual leader of The Brotherhood, a Hindu religious organization

Juan Garcia—Vishal Patel's chauffeur

Martin—a waiter at The Dock

Justin—a worker at Ledacorp

The Asshole—producer of pornography who works in the graffiti building

Father Tim McNally—owner of the church building

ITALICIZED INTRODUCTION

In Ayodhya, India, under the Trinity of Gods, Bhen relaxed palathi, awaiting her favorite devotee.

Narendra got on his knees, his palms together, and bowed in respect.

Bhen held up her own palm, blessing him.

"What message shall I take with me to America, mata?" he asked.

"Justice and equality, my son," she said. "Teach your children well."

PRELUDE

Union Square was finally quiet. Four a.m., when even the homeless quit the streets.

Priya, tears streaming down her face, wearing her favorite panjabi, stared down as if the street was an abyss rather than a sign of promise. Once, it had seemed that way; once, she had watched enviously at the women swaying down the street with their Prada bags.

One person could take it away from her. But she knew she'd already taken it away from herself.

The long journey down didn't seem as empty as her future—or as void as her soul.

PART I

1

Niral boarded the bus outside his house in Fresh Meadows, heading toward the Brotherhood meeting at the public school in downtown Flushing. He made his way to the back of the bus, playing with his janoi string through the top of his shirt, when he saw an old friend, Wan. He looked ten years older, with extra tattoos and devoid of his swirly Korean hairdo.

"Wan? You're out?" Niral asked.

"Niral! Just got out of the House and who do I run into? My nigga."

"Thought they gave you life for killing that cabby?"

"Ten to life, nigga. Good behavior got me out. I even got Ricky sending money to his widow. That's how the system reforms you."

"Glad you help your people out before exploiting them."

Wan smiled. "How about you? What you been up to since high school?"

Niral didn't have time to explain it: his decision not to attend college—even though he'd graduated from an elite public high school; the years of struggle writing bad novels in Bushwick; the crazy sex parties at Jeremy's loft in the East Village; hooking up with random girls and feeling empty and wasted; waking up in Chloe's shower with blood and mucus congealed on his chest; and finally realizing his father had been right: he'd been living a lie.

Art. God.

No point in explaining because he had changed. He was trying to be better. Stan Lorenzo, his father's friend from the NYPD, would help him become an investigator if Niral would help himself.

"Nothing, man. I'm working an office job in Long Island City. Filing divorce cases."

"You should come by the spa," Wan replied. "That's where I'm staying with Ricky. Right past the Korean church. Flushing's changed, but not too much. Just got a nice shipment of illegal Korean girls, young and fresh, straight from the motherland. Usually you need a password and you gotta be Korean, but I give my friends free rides. And if you want out of the divorce game, trust me: I can get you a good gig."

Dilipuncle stood outside the elementary school make of old red brick, wearing a gray suit and red tie. He smiled as Niral approached.

"Niral! I have heard you believe again in Bhen!"

Niral nodded.

"Don't you feel bad. We all stray from the true path. Before my wife died, I didn't believe in Bhen either; I would just come to Brotherhood meetings because Kirti wanted me to. But then, Narendrabhai showed me the way. So did Amrat."

"How's he? And Priya?"

"He is good. Amrat quit Harvard after Kirti died. He got a degree in computer engineering, and he works for the city now. Priya is at NYU." Dilipuncle smiled. "Stern Business School."

"She lives in the East Village?"

"Yes, in a dormitory on 14th Street."

Niral remembered his old haunt like it was yesterday.

"Yes, it's a nice neighborhood," he said bitterly. "How's work?"

Dilipuncle shook his head. "Accounting...numbers are boring. I think I will retire soon. But Amrat will carry on. He pays for Priya. He is a very good son. Ever since Kirti died, he helps me with the mortgage too. Even with all these housing collapses, people refinancing...we never have to. Amrat is so reliable."

They entered, took off their shoes, and sat inside the school auditorium, on the side for males. In front of the trinity of Gods and a small portrait of

Bhen, Narendrakaka, the head of the North American chapter of the Hindu organization, the Brotherhood, stood alongside Niral's father and led the prayer.

Afterwards, he announced that Shri Holi, an event to celebrate the Hindu holiday featuring plays and dances, would be held in a couple of weeks, and that Donation Night, where true devotees could donate to the Brotherhood Fund, would be held in a few days at Niral's house. Unfortunately, Niral couldn't donate yet because only true devotees who didn't expect anything in return were allowed to make donations. Niral wasn't yet considered a true devotee.

Niral, sleeping in his parents' basement—now his apartment—woke up suddenly. It was six a.m. He had been having a nightmare about the morning he woke up in Chloe's shower and saw a vision of Brahma commanding him to return home. He thought all that crazy stuff was behind him, but as his father approached his bed, a concerned look on his face, Niral sensed he might soon be in a nightmare within a nightmare.

He was right. His father stood in the distance, like a prophet engulfed in shadow, and told him something unthinkable had happened, something that could change their lives. Priya Mehta had killed herself by jumping out of a NYU dorm building at four that morning.

During the next few days, Niral cleared his mind by visiting his friend Rob in Westchester. Rob was an Australian drifter who had hung out with Niral, Jeremy, and Chloe in the East Village until he got a gig upstate. They canoed on the Hudson River, something Niral considered both relaxing and challenging, considering he couldn't swim very well due to his inner-city upbringing. Wearing his life jacket as they floated over a mile of water made him feel simultaneously both protected and vulnerable.

When he returned from his short vacation, he was forced to face the reality of his community's situation. His father told him that Priya's brother, Amrat, had gone berserk, telling people in the Brotherhood that she'd been murdered, something even more unthinkable in the Indian-American community than suicide.

The case was being investigated by Detective Savard, a detective Niral's father knew well, and all the evidence indicated suicide. Inside her dorm room, the police found no fingerprints or DNA of anyone but her roommate Jody Chou, who had stayed the night with her boyfriend and only found out about the death when she'd been woken up by the police. No witnesses actually saw her jump, just a few had heard her hit the sidewalk: a homeless lady on her way back to her shelter and a young couple returning to their Alphabet City apartment after a tryst in the Union Square park. The couple had called the cops, who had found her room locked from the inside. Her hallmates hadn't woken up or seen anyone, and no one had signed in or out with the guard downstairs.

Inside his living room, under the portraits of the trinity of Gods, Niral spoke with his father and Narendrakaka.

"Priya was like our daughter," Narendrakaka said. "Never has this happened before in our community."

"Stanuncle has made Niral responsible," Niral's father said. "He is a good boy now, dedicated to the Brotherhood. He will investigate for us."

"Prakashbhai, I hope so," Narendrakaka said. "The police will do nothing. Didn't you work with this detective once?

"Yes, but I was never a detective. Savard may listen to Stanuncle. Remember, after seventy-two hours, they consider the case closed. They have already ruled it a suicide. Now they will not waste their time without further evidence or pressure from the outside."

"No Indian would commit suicide," Narendrakaka said. "It is against God, an act of cowardice."

Niral's father turned to his son. "Amrat will be visiting you tomorrow. He is crushed by Priya's death. Remember to be gentle with him."

Niral nodded deferentially. He hoped that his work and obedience would allow him to one day save money and donate to the Brotherhood Fund.

He bowed to his father, prostrating himself, and his father responded by planting his palm firmly on Niral's head.

"Make us proud, son."

PART II

Niral leaned against a gas pipe in the Lorenzo Investigations' conference room, watching through the window at porn stars smoking, many with black circles around their eyes. Their hands twitched as they waited to be led into a place he termed the graffiti building by an asshole who dressed the same way all asshole guys dressed—in an untucked black dress shirt and khakis.

In the main room of Lorenzo's Long Island City office, Stan was chatting on the phone with a typical client, a wronged wife who wanted the dirt on her husband so she could exploit New York's ancient at-fault divorce laws and seize half his assets.

Stan agreed to keep his car under surveillance to see if her husband, Bob Macaday—a mick-turned-aristocrat who'd married a shrewish Jew—was picking up chicks. They'd gone to her mansion in Forest Hills, cracked into his computer, and placed cameras in non-private places. They snooped around in drawers for letters but found nothing. Still, the wife insisted he was cheating, and like in retail, the client was always right.

Stan finished up the phone call and summoned Niral inside.

"Can you finish up the bookkeeping when you get a chance?" he asked Niral.

"Should I pay the rent too?"

"I'll take care of it," Stan answered. "Just enter the payments, calculate the float, and deposit the checks."

Strange, Niral thought, *a few months of not paying the rent*. But he didn't have time to ponder because there was a knock on the door, a grave tap. A black shroud appeared through the translucent glass. When Niral opened the door, he recognized the round face and majestic forehead with the holy dot at the center.

"She would never have killed herself," Amrat said, glaring across the conference room table at Niral. "She had too much honor."

Stan sat adjacent to Niral with pencil and yellow notepad.

Priya's urn rested in front of Amrat. Priya's wake and cremation had taken place while Niral had been in Westchester visiting Rob, and now her brother had brought her ashes with him, hoping to persuade his childhood acquaintance to investigate her death.

"Don't you usually throw the ashes in the river?" Niral asked.

"Until this situation is resolved, I will preserve them," Amrat responded.

"You've never been one for tradition," Niral said. Amrat glared at him severely.

"It has been a while, Niral. I've changed a lot. But this is a special situation."

Stan tapped his pencil against the pad, listening to them impatiently.

"Normally, I wouldn't go near a murder or suicide," he interrupted. "Didn't go any farther than larceny when I was in the department. Now that I'm retired, I've got even less of a bent. But Niral's dad, Prak, is my man, and Niral needs experience, so you've got him at your beck and call as long as my fee's paid."

"You will get your money, Mr. Lorenzo. I saved much for Priya's college, even graduate school."

"That's fine. But if things get too heated, I'm gonna pull the plug. I talked to Detective Savard; he says he's got no evidence. If she didn't kill herself, do you have any theories on what happened?"

"I don't know, but I believe Vishal was involved."

"Who's he?"

"Niral's friend," Amrat said.

"He's not my friend," Niral corrected, responding to Stan's puzzled stare, "but we all knew him from when we were kids."

"He was dating Priya," Amrat continued. "I ran into them at a restaurant the night she died."

"You told the police this?" Stan asked.

"They believe it's a suicide, so they didn't take my story seriously. They rely too much on science these days."

"Guess I've been out of the department for a while," Stan said.

"Before that night, I did not know they were seeing one another. We fought, I must admit. But they left the restaurant together, and that is the last time I saw her."

"Or maybe," Niral said, "she was upset that you found her with a forbidden squeeze."

Amrat smashed his fist against the table and rose, shaking furiously.

Niral jumped up and grabbed Amrat's skinny yet strong shoulders. Amrat's eyes were wide, and the whites of his eyes had reddened.

"Okay," Stan said, standing too, holding his palms out. "Chill out. Trust us. Niral will work on it."

7

"Did you ever think, Niral, that any of us would have this view?" Vishal asked, pointing out from the balcony of his seventy-seventh floor apartment in Murray Hill. He was staring at the Pepsi-Cola sign across the East River in Long Island City.

"I never wanted it," Niral said.

"Come on," Vishal continued. "I told you way back, bohemianism was dead; capitalism would reign. Did you listen? Now you got your dad's job. Hell, lower than that, a fucking assistant to some pathetic PI, hanging out in the hood I stare down on every night."

"It's a job. I'm trying to do better."

"How long will it take you to become a PI?"

"Three years."

Vishal slapped Niral's back, then put his arm around his shoulder.

"In three years, dude, if you work for me, you'll be living in a pad like this, you'll have a mansion in Westchester and a helipad on Sands Point. That's how long it took me to learn Carty's trade, steal his clients, and rise against the housing collapse. While my clients made grade, his ass fell off the radar. Now Carty's somewhere in Montana trying to hide from the douches who lost out. Amazing how things work."

"You're proud of becoming rich off the misery of others?"

"Everything's a gamble. I made a good gamble. You made a bad gamble. But you've got a second chance because you have a safety net. It's called The Brotherhood. Those rich white kids wouldn't help you, but the

Brotherhood will. I will. You think my dad's living off his retirement? Only reason he's still working in that deli in Jackson Heights is because he's got pride. Otherwise he'd be in Florida now. I bought a house there just for him."

"Benevolent of you."

"Yeah, and I've got more. I donate to the Brotherhood Fund, to other philanthropic causes. I do good."

Niral looked at him angrily. Vishal laughed.

"Come inside; have some Sazerac," he said.

Vishal slid the glass door open, and they entered an enormous living room shaped like an egg. They passed his sixty-inch TV and leather couch. He opened the latch on his minibar and removed some liquor.

"You remember Meetal?"

"Your sister?"

"U. Chicago. Northwestern Journalism School. An idiot like you. What's she going to write, a blog? Perfect match."

"Is she in New York?"

"Yup. Back for spring break. Holi. She's here for good starting in the summer."

Vishal held two shot glasses filled with brown liquid and handed one to Niral.

"Let's talk about another idiot," Niral said, lightly sipping the nectar. "Priya."

Vishal's smile became a frown. He turned away from Niral and treaded back toward the minibar.

"I'll pretend you didn't say that," he said, opening the minibar again.

"You loved her?" Niral asked.

He shut the door with force.

"What do you think?"

"What happened that night, Vishal?"

Approaching Niral, the Sazerac sloshing in his glass, Vishal pointed at Niral's face.

"That jerk Amrat ruined our romantic dinner at The Dock, that's what."

"He didn't know about you guys?"

"Would you tell that freak? Priya and I were good together. She was studying finance too."

"A college kid."

"She was in grad school, man. A few years younger. Like you dating Meetal. And she was mature for her age. She understood the world, unlike her brother."

"What happened?"

"He made a scene. Got himself kicked out. We didn't feel like sticking around after that. The Dock's on the other side of the East River, in your hood, so we took the boat across, then I dropped her off in my limo. Front of the building."

"Was she upset?"

"Fuck yeah. How would you feel if Amrat was your brother? She was probably scared he was going to cut her up. God, I feel like pulverizing him."

"Do you believe she killed herself?"

"I don't want to believe it. But if you're investigating it for Amrat, I suggest you look at your taskmaster instead. Think about it, what was Amrat doing there? He doesn't even go to restaurants."

The phone rang, and Vishal picked up. Niral realized that Vishal was right. His father had told him that since Amrat's conversion from atheism in college after his mother passed away, he rarely ever ate out, choosing to follow Gandhi's dictum of self-reliance.

"Yeah, tell her to come up," Vishal ordered into the landline and hung up. He turned his attention back to Niral.

"I've got a guest. Sorry, I have to cut this short. But remember what I told you. Imbed it in your memory."

"About Amrat and the restaurant?"

"About my investment firm. Visit us downtown, man. I'll show you the ropes, and you'll never have to be in Long Island City again, unless it's at The Dock or maybe chilling in a condo I build."

8

The doorbell rang. When Vishal opened the door, Niral saw a gorgeous brunette with thick lips wearing a low-cut tank top, jean shorts, and a light jacket. She glanced quickly at Vishal, then smiled at Niral.

"Niral, Lauren," Vishal announced, waving lazily. They shook hands. Niral tried to take his eyes off her but couldn't.

"Do I know you from somewhere?" Niral asked.

Lauren shrugged. "I don't think so."

"Not in your league, bro," Vishal said. "Unless you went to Yale with us."

Vishal hit him on the back. Niral swallowed, embarrassed.

"Niral here is a homegrown bohemian," Vishal said.

"Is that right?" Lauren asked, touching Niral's elbow. "I'm not too big on degrees myself."

"Lauren's an artist. Moronic, but at least she went to Yale first."

"Vishal can be such a snob," she responded.

"Well, I should go," Niral said reluctantly, trying to avoid looking at Lauren as he left the apartment. But as he descended the building on the elevator, he vaguely remembered someone who looked like Lauren smoking a cigarette outside the graffiti building one afternoon. He knew artists lived there along with the porn filmmakers, and they usually came out around the same time the girls took a break for their hits.

Downstairs, he stopped at the security desk.

"Can you do me a favor and tell me the full name of the person who just went up to 7742?"

The guard was a middle-aged black man. He didn't move or respond. He just stared at Niral, dumbfounded.

"Uh, no," he finally intoned. "Unless you're Vishal Patel."

"I am Vishal Patel."

"Mister, I know Vishal Patel. You for damn sure ain't Vishal Patel."

Niral, frustrated, shook his head.

"I'm his friend. I just went up to see him. You called up for me, remember? I met that girl when I was up there. She told me her name but I forgot it on the way down. That's why I'm asking."

"You know the way back up, sir. Otherwise, I can't help you."

Niral started walking back to the elevator. Suddenly, he stopped and, deciding to try a different tactic, backed up and leaned in on the guard. "Look," he said, "I used to work security myself. Now I'm a PI." He took out his Lorenzo's Investigations business card and gave it to the guard.

"That ain't no license," the guard responded, flipping it back at Niral. "I know plenty of PIs. I got friends that are PIs, and you ain't no PI."

"How do you know that?" Niral asked, picking up the card.

"Because they don't make rookie mistakes like this. Now get out of here before I report you for impersonation."

Niral put the card back in his pocket and smacked a twenty on the table. The guard laughed.

"That's your angle? Mr. Patel tips me a hundred just for opening the door. You're in the wrong league, kid."

9

Niral cursed himself as he jaywalked across the street, avoiding the steaming manholes. He paced in front of a dreary, red-tinged bar, replaying the incident in his mind.

Then, deciding to forget it and form a plan of action, he entered the bar and decided to wait for Lauren. She was probably unimportant to the investigation, but he found it strange that Vishal was hanging out with an artist who lived in the graffiti building, if that was her.

Vishal treated Niral like dirt simply because he hadn't gone to college. Only now that he had rejoined the Brotherhood community and wished to change himself into a responsible person did Vishal want Niral to work for him, and he wondered if Vishal had an angle on Lauren too or if they were lovers.

He stayed near the window so he could monitor the front of Vishal's building. He tried to zone out his surroundings: yelling, drunken college kids and financial analysts. After being hassled by the bartender, he ordered a beer, but he kept it at an arm's length and pretended to sip it only to keep up appearances.

Twenty minutes later, after he had almost lost patience and was about to head toward the subway, Lauren emerged, dressed the same, but this time carrying a black leather bag on her shoulder.

She immediately took a left toward FDR Drive. Niral left the bar and followed about fifty yards behind her.

She crossed the street, slipped under the expressway, walked between a couple of NYPD trailers and, taking another left, approached the pier, where a boat laid waiting.

A tall white man guarded the pier. He was about to hook a chain across the entrance, but he made an exception as he saw Lauren hurrying up the boardwalk. He smiled at her and appeared to make a joke. She smacked him on the arm and, as he laughed, climbed aboard a boat tied to the pier.

Quickly, the man hooked the chain and followed behind her. Niral started to run, but the boat undocked immediately and zoomed in a diagonal trajectory toward the Queensboro Bridge on the other side of the East River.

As he approached the chain, Niral stopped, panting. He watched the boat recede into the distance. Standing between the trailers and watching the river, Niral's heart beat fast. As he was about to leave, he noticed a sign indicating the pier exclusively hosted a boat for customers wishing to dine at The Dock.

10

The next morning, Niral strolled along Union Square, his old haunt of adventures he was trying to forget. As he approached Priya's former NYU residence, he could still see splotches of blood stamped on the pavement from her fall, like a footprint of death. He figured he'd probably bled or thrown up on the same spot many times before.

Entering the building, he gave his name to the security guard, a burly black woman who glared at him suspiciously as she called up to Priya's roommate, Jody Chou.

A few minutes later, Niral peered out Priya's window, noticing how many windows in the opposing building faced it. Somebody could have seen a struggle, even at four in the morning.

He had read the police report and was surprised only a few people in that building had been interviewed. One would hope that if someone had seen something, they would have reported it, so perhaps the oversight didn't matter. Then again, this was New York, so there were no guarantees.

Jody sat uncomfortably in her Winnie the Pooh pajamas on her neatly-made Winnie the Pooh covered bed. Directly across from her was Priya's bed, now totally stripped to the bare mattress. Niral noticed Jody's shirt barely constrained her large breasts. He tried not to look at them as he interrogated her.

"Is there any way to get into the building other than through the front door? It seemed pretty secure. Is it like that at night?"

"There's always a guard there. It's annoying if someone wants to visit you. I heard it wasn't so bad before September 11th. But there is another way in. An emergency exit in the back. It leads up to a dead end, but a fire escape's there, and you can climb up. Sometimes kids go out to smoke; sometimes they leave it open and anyone can get in."

"Did you tell the cops that when they interviewed you?"

"They said there was no evidence anyone was in here, so I didn't mention it."

"When did you see Priya last?"

"Six o'clock that night. She was getting ready, putting on makeup, when I left to go to Matt's apartment a couple of blocks away."

"Did you see Vishal?"

"Who's Vishal?"

"You don't know him? He was her boyfriend."

"Honestly, I wouldn't know. All I know is, since October, sometimes a Hispanic guy would pick her up in a black limo."

"How often?"

"Twice a week, sometimes more. She never told me anything. We used to be best friends, but sometime in October she really changed. She stopped talking to me, and she'd take her calls in the bathroom."

"So you girls were friends?"

"We used to be besties. We were so excited to be rooming together. In undergrad she lived at home, but she talked her brother into letting her live at school for grad. We both wanted to be financial analysts. We were happy when we got into Stern and felt even luckier to get student housing as grad students. You know how much my boyfriend pays for rent just a couple of blocks away?"

"Yeah, I know."

"It's crazy. Priya and me, we wanted banker guys, both of us, and when I found my guy, Matt, I felt bad for her, so I kept setting her up with Matt's friends. First, I tried white guys, then she said she was sick of dating white guys. So, I tried the Indian guys, and they were all finance guys too, but she said she wasn't too into any of them either. Maybe the whole i-banking collapse scared her, I don't know.

"Then one day she just changed. She got cold. She started screaming at me if I left clothes on her bed, even though she never cared before. I tried to talk to her about it, but she'd just tell me to leave her alone and give her space. So I did. I started spending more time at Matt's place, so I don't really know what went on here."

"I guess you weren't completely surprised she killed herself?"

"Something was definitely wrong with her. I just didn't know what."

"Did you ever see a tall Indian guy visit her?"

"Doesn't sound like anyone I remember, unless it was one of the finance guys she dated, but like I said, she wasn't into them, and I don't remember any of them coming over, unless it was when I was out. Her brother would come over sometimes to fix things, like her computer. I guess he's some kind of computer engineer along with being a guru or whatever."

"You didn't like him?"

"I didn't dislike him, but he was strange. I thought he ran Priya's life too much. Way too nosy. But I have to say, he did help us install this ceiling fan. Apparently against University regulations since I'm getting fined for it. Meanwhile, I can't get a room transfer; campus housing is booked, so I'm either stuck in this death pad or at Matt's place."

"Did you see Priya and Amrat get into a fight?"

"She was pretty quiet around him. He definitely ran things. Her dad came by once in a while too, and they seemed to get along well. He brought her chocolates, nice dresses, and jewelry and stuff, and even waited outside the room while she was changing, saying he wanted to be respectful of her space, and then he took her out to a nice dinner. With her brother, she just stuck by his side, nodding and saying yes or no. He did come by once after she died, to get the rest of the stuff the cops hadn't taken. Just some clothing and stuff in the drawers."

Niral slid them open and saw they were empty. Then he excused himself and made his way to the fire escape. Carefully, he descended down the skeleton stairs, until he reached a slightly open window, which he slid up and went under, then proceeded down the solid stairs to the emergency exit.

Sure enough, the door was propped open. He heard some skinny white kids chatting outside and smelled some sweet smoke linger in. He snooped around, and in the corner, next to an unemptied trashcan, saw a crumpled red and gold odhni, a scarf-like cloth normally worn with a panjabi or sari. Kneeling down, he observed a large, dark red stain on it, possibly blood.

He called Detective Savard, who came over within ten minutes and secured the odhni.

"Good work, kid. We'll put it into the grinder and see what happens. How's Stan?"

"The same, I guess."

"I don't know if your old man told you, but we used to call him 'Stan the man.' He used to get all the chicks at the cop bars. We don't know how he did it. I guess that's how he got married twice and divorced twice. Now he's just got his work."

"I don't know much about him. He doesn't really share his personal life with me."

"Ever wonder why he's friends with your dad?"

"I called him Stanuncle when I was little. He was just another elder, but he happened to be white. Now I'm not sure what he is to me."

"Your dad's something. He'd never even curse around us. He was on the beat, so I didn't see him around too much, but I worked with him at the 110. Crazy Corona."

"He says he's kind of ashamed of those years. He just wants to be a sanyasi now, someone who renounces worldly desires."

Savard shook his head. "Well, wish him luck for me," he said.

Niral returned to Long Island City. He got off the 7 train and passed Tony's Diner. He said hi to Ole, the guard for the church building, and took the elevator up to the office. In the hallway, the custodian of the building, Lance, was vacuuming.

"Brother Niral," he said. "Wanna come with me on an adventure?"

"I told you, Lance," Niral responded as he put in the key, "I'm not into that anymore."

"Queens Boulevard, man. That's where the action's at. I told you, I'm CEO; I'll get the girls. I give you a promotion too, but you gotta earn it."

"It's all right. I'll take a raincheck."

"Stan was my partner in the game way back when, but now he says he's too old. You're the new recruit. You change your mind, I'll be down at Tony's, grabbing a burger for lunch."

Niral waved him away, locked the door from the inside, and went directly to the conference room window to gaze at the girls.

It was lunchtime, so the artsy chicks outnumbered the porn girls. But he didn't see Lauren.

He returned to his desk and turned on the computer to write some notes on the investigation so far. On the keyboard, Niral saw a note from Stan, informing him Stan was doing car surveillance that night on Mr. Macaday. If he wanted to come along, he could meet him around six in Forest Hills. But if Niral was too busy with the Amrat case, Stan could do it without him.

For the first time, Stan had showed real confidence in him. Usually he commanded, but now he gave Niral a choice. First, to take this case, now, this option. Better than bookkeeping and sitting next to Stan in the car pointing the long lens at a suit with his pants down.

Niral wrote some notes on the investigation. The odhni was a big break. He realized he should have reminded Savard to interview some more people in the opposite building, though he could go himself the next day. He still needed to check out The Dock, too, and see if the waiters recalled what had happened that night.

He wrote an email to Savard, then completed some of the bookkeeping. He entered the payments from clients into the accounting software, printed out checks for bills and put them into proper envelopes, then transferred the remaining float into another account, printed a check as two weeks' payment to himself and another to deposit into the company bank account. He noticed again that the rent hadn't been paid in a few months. He knew Stan always begged Father Tim McNally, the Catholic priest who managed the office building for a church a few blocks away, for extra time paying, and Tim usually let him. Maybe he was paying for it with his own funds, Niral thought. He could check Stan's personal Quickbooks account, but on second thought, he decided it was none of his business.

He opened the door to head down to the bank, but Mrs. Macaday stood in his way. She was a tall, blonde white woman, wearing a black dress and pearls around her neck. She always wore an expression of outrage.

"Where's Mr. Lorenzo?" she asked.

"Not here," Niral responded.

"He knows he has to follow Bob tonight, right?"

"Yes."

"Are you sure?"

"He left me a note."

"I just hope he doesn't give the job to you."

"He's going to do it himself."

"Thank God. I was just at Tiffany's and I thought I would stop by to make sure. Otherwise I wouldn't be caught dead in this neighborhood. You know there are actual drug addicts here?"

"Some are of that opinion."

"It's disgusting. Girls wasting their lives. I just hope the mayor does something about this. Every time he's on the news, he says there's no crime anymore. Please."

Niral continued to stand there, trying to be patient as she seemed to fumble for something inside her large purse.

"My mace," she said, taking it out. "I haven't used it since the '80s, but I still keep it around."

She waved it in Niral's face. He tried not to scowl.

"Anyway," she said, raising her nose as she dropped the mace into her bag, where it landed with a pop, "you will see me after this is done, I suppose. Remember to tell Mr. Lorenzo that I stopped by."

She turned mechanically and headed to the elevator. Niral waited until she was inside and away before he followed down the stairs.

13

As he passed Tony's, Niral noticed Lauren outside the graffiti building, so he ducked inside the diner. Lance raised his arm, and Niral joined him at the window seat.

"Just about finished with lunch. What took you so long?"

"I had no choice."

"Damn right. This company recruits the best talent. Just see if we can't find some fine ladies for some staff positions."

Niral covered the window-side of his face with his hand.

"You ain't gonna recruit by playing spy, man. What, the sun's too strong for you?"

"I'm trying to avoid that girl."

"What girl?" Lance asked, glancing toward the building. "Oh shit! I know her."

"You've see her outside before?"

"I seen her inside, in premium positions. That's Cherry. Schoolgirl at Gigglies on Queens Boulevard. Only nude club in the city."

"Are you sure? I'm pretty sure she went to Yale."

"Economy's that bad, I guess. That's why we need to up this enterprise. She needs some better work, and we better give it to her."

Lauren finished her cigarette, ground it down with her heel, and waited at the door until the black-shirted asshole opened it for her and let her inside, scanning her body until she disappeared, then turning toward the rabble and calling girls for the afternoon porn shoots.

"I have to go," Niral announced, getting up.

"Not hungry?"

"I have a date later."

"Since when?"

"Last night. She called me."

"Then you go, brother. But take my advice, don't get too close, or else you'll get burned like me and Stan and all those guys you investigate. Once she gets in your pocket, it never ends. Alimony up the wazoo. You'll be working two full-time jobs to make ends meet, still trying to raise your punk kid right while she's talking shit to you and hanging out with assholes. Believe me."

"I'll keep your advice in mind," Niral said, turning to leave.

"Listen, Niral, after eleven, I got off till the early morning. I'll be here at Tony's and then off to Queens Boulevard if you wanna come with. I need a CFO."

"I'll think about it," Niral replied, shaking his head as he turned and left.

After depositing checks in the bank, Niral bought a falafel and returned to his office. It was true: Meetal had called him the night before as he was on the subway home and said she wanted to meet him for an early dinner near Vishal's office on Wall Street.

Once he got back, he seated himself at his desk and took out the falafel, the tahini sauce dripping off the wax wrapper, and munched a few bites. Then he started a new Word file and typed out questions he had so far regarding the investigation:

1) Could a killer have entered the building via the back exit, struggled with Priya, and dropped the odhni as he left?

2) Why hadn't he left any DNA evidence?

3) Why hadn't Priya's roommate seen Vishal?

4) Why had Priya changed in October?

5) Why had Amrat been at that restaurant?

6) Why was Vishal friends with a stripper?

He finished his meal and noticed the tahini sauce had dripped on his shirt, so he wiped it off with a wet tissue. Then after cleaning his hands, he pondered his questions and realized he could resolve some by talking to Vishal when he went down to Wall Street. And given it was time to get going, he put the computer to sleep, headed out of the office and toward the subway.

Vishal's company on Wall Street, LedaCorp, had an office on the thirty-fourth floor of a large office building facing the Statue of Liberty and a large swath of Staten Island. Niral went through the usual sign-in and call up process, and when the elevator doors slid open, he was automatically within the company confines. Past a secretary's desk was a large room lined with computers where mostly young guys were perched over their desks or haggling over spreadsheets. A large ticker board displayed company signs and numbers Niral could barely understand.

Vishal emerged and welcomed him into his office to the side of the computer room.

"What do you think?" he asked, leading Niral to a cushioned leather chair.

"Doesn't seem as glamorous as I imagined," Niral replied, plopping down.

"There's no glamour in work," Vishal said. "All the glamour's outside of work."

"Isn't that the opposite of what Marx said?"

"Did you take European History at that community college of yours?"

"I wanted to ask you more about Priya."

"Happy subjects. Shoot."

"You ever meet her roommate, Jody?"

Vishal made himself comfortable behind his desk.

"What kind of a question is that?"

"Just a question."

"No," he said carefully. "I never had the pleasure."

"Just seems odd you dated her and never met the person she lived with."

"I guess we were kind of odd. But it comes back to our favorite person, Amrat. Priya didn't want him to find out, so we hid the relationship as much as possible."

"A black limo. A Hispanic guy?"

"My chauffeur, Juan. Back to my place. Routine."

"And Priya never seemed upset about anything?"

"That her insane brother would find out and rip out her heart? No, other than that, nothing."

Before Niral could ask him about Lauren, he heard a shrill and excited voice shout out his name.

Turning, he saw a beautiful, light-skinned Indian girl enter wearing a pink dress.

"Oh, hey!" Niral said, getting up.

"It's been so long!" Meetal replied, standing there awkwardly, her arms halfway out. Then, when the right moment came, she leapt forward to give Niral a hug. Niral laughed despite himself and padded her lightly on the back.

"A family reunion," Vishal commented, coming around the desk. "See what delights you receive when you come over here, Niral? Just the beginning, my friend, just the beginning."

16

They hadn't picked a restaurant. Since they were both veggies now, Vishal suggested an Italian place close by. As they left the building with Vishal, Niral noticed his limo. It was similar to the one Jody described. A young Hispanic male waited at the driver's side.

Vishal said he had a dinner date, but he offered them a ride to the restaurant. Meetal kissed her brother on the cheek and, clasping Niral's arm in her own, respectfully declined.

While getting in the limo, Vishal pointed in the direction of the restaurant.

Niral was nervous. It had been a long time since his last date.

Meetal's cheeriness calmed him down. As they strolled toward the restaurant, they talked about their past lives as teenagers, when Meetal knew Niral as her brother's intellectual friend.

"I was so shocked that you didn't go to college after Tech."

"Yeah, I hear that a lot."

"I don't mean it negatively. It was actually pretty bold."

"Not the way your brother tells it."

"Vishal is Vishal. What can you do? He sees the world through his lens."

"What's your lens?"

"I like to think a more accurate one."

"An inclusive one?"

"To start."

They entered the restaurant, were seated and ordered. They talked a bit about their lives after their teenage years. Niral told her about his failed attempts at writing books, leaving out his disastrous experiments with sex and drugs. Meetal mentioned she studied Bharat Natyam in college, and that she was going to perform a dance later in the week for a Brotherhood function in honor of the Holi festival.

Then she grew quiet. Niral noticed tears trickle down her face, and she began to weep for real.

"What's wrong?" he asked, reaching over to her.

"Just thinking about Priya. She was so young."

"Were you guys close?"

"We hadn't talked since our Brotherhood days. I still remember, we would hang out after class and talk about the cute guys who would play basketball in the gym. We'd trade notes on dance and drama and stuff."

"Did you know she was dating Vishal?"

"Yes, he told me."

"When?"

"I don't know, maybe in October."

He nodded. Then he began tapping the table with his finger, thinking about the implications of this as the waiter delivered his rigatoni with marinara sauce and Meetal's tortellini alfredo. As she watched him, Meetal's expression changed into one of anger and annoyance.

"Tell me something: are you interviewing me?" she asked.

"What?" Niral said, like he'd woken from a reverie.

"Vishal told me you were looking into Priya's death for that creep Amrat."

"Yeah, so what?"

40

"We're supposed to be getting to know each other. We're not in some interrogation room."

Niral extended his arms, his palms facing Meetal.

"Hey, you called me. I don't need to defend myself."

Meetal stood up fast, almost knocking against a waiter who was passing.

"I can't believe you, Niral Solanke. You tricked me."

"I didn't," he said. "It just came up. You're making a big deal out of a few questions?"

"Look, my brother had nothing to do with it. If you knew him, if you talked to him, you'd know that."

"I never said he did. We're just having dinner."

Meetal started crying again. She paced around a couple of times, then escaped into the bathroom. When she returned, her tears had dried, and she was breathing regularly.

"Okay, maybe I overreacted," she said. "I guess I'm kind of nervous. I dated white guys in college, and now I just don't know what to do."

"It's okay."

"No, it's not," she said. "I was unfair."

She began eating her tortellini. Niral started thinking again.

"Priya dated a lot of white guys, too, before Vishal," he said.

Meetal's eyes widened. She put down her fork and got up again.

"I'm going," she said.

"Are you serious?" Niral asked, rising to meet her.

"I'm sorry, Niral, I can't do this. I'm too high-strung, and you asking questions..."

"I don't understand, Meetal."

"Just forget it," she said. "Date Amrat if you want."

She stormed out of the restaurant. Niral followed her for a bit, calling out to her as she marched down the street. But she entered the subway, and he gave up.

17

He strolled down Wall Street, then walked all the way to Battery Park, trying to think of what went wrong. He had been shocked when Meetal had called, but also pleasantly surprised. He hadn't really dated a girl since Zaineb, a rich Muslim NYU student from Connecticut who'd broken his heart when she'd decided she would rather be a guy who was destined to be a corporate lawyer. Then trysts with random girls at parties and with Chloe. This date had been a step up for him, part of his resurgent new self in the Brotherhood. Yet this also had gone wrong.

He tried to think about what he should do now. It was too late to join Stan in Forest Hills and the surveillance of Mr. Macaday. He still hadn't gone to The Dock to interview the workers there about what they had seen, so he figured that was a logical step.

He took the subway up to Murray Hill and walked over to Vishal's apartment. He figured it was better to retrace the steps Priya would have taken rather than going over to Long Island City and finding the place that way, if there was a way.

He passed Vishal's apartment building, saw the same guard inside, then strolled under FDR Drive. He turned back and looked up to find Vishal's apartment, but there were too many for him to deduce which was his. He continued toward the water and slipped between the police trailers, which were empty as usual.

The boat was docked, the string unlatched. He climbed aboard the pier and boarded the boat. He was joined by a crew of white college kids, two guys wearing tuxedos and one girl in a tight black dress and light jacket. She was smoking a cigarette despite the clear sign above her head banning it as she leaned out over the water and complained about her overbearing stepmother. She reminded Niral of Chloe, so he stayed on the opposite side of the boat, holding onto a pole as his stomach lurched from the boat rocking back and forth. Then, he felt the surge as the boat sped toward the other side of the East River, the wind fiercer than anything on the Hudson.

18

When he exited the boat, he immediately asked the maître d' if she would get the manager. A young man wearing a vest approached him and escorted him past elderly patrons dining at closely placed tables covered with white linen and into a small office next to a hallway.

Inside the office sat a balding, middle-aged white man with a large scar across his left cheek, wearing a blue dress shirt. He was punching numbers on a calculator. Papers were stacked up on the floors of the office, and a pristine picture of the man's family—his wife, daughter, and dog in a suburban setting with a white fence—lay on his desk. The man glanced up quickly and nodded for Niral to sit on a wooden chair, which creaked under Niral's weight.

"May I help you?" he asked with an Italian-American accent.

Niral took out his card and placed it on the desk.

"I'm a private investigator. I'm looking into the death of a girl who ate here last week."

The manager glanced at the card. "When exactly?"

"Thursday."

The manager picked up the calculator and repositioned it to his right. He checked a calendar pasted onto the desk.

"I wasn't here. My assistant, Martin, was."

He called the other man back. Niral explained what had taken place that Thursday night and asked if Martin had seen it.

"There was a brief altercation," he said. "Some crazy Indian guy yelling at some poor girl. I remember it."

"Do you recall what he said?"

"He said something about her being a slut, hooking up with her cousin or something. I came by just as they were dragging the guy out, so I'm not sure."

"Do you remember who else was with her?"

Martin didn't answer at first. He seemed to be looking to his manager for instructions, but the manager just stared back at him coldly.

"Her and some guy," Martin finally replied. "I didn't know them. They were having dinner with another couple, I think."

"Was one of them a white brunette?"

"I'm not sure, man," he said. Niral noticed he was sweating. "It all happened fast. I was in the office until my waiters called me out."

"Are those waiters here today?"

"No. We've got a lot of waiters. They come in and out."

The manager rose and hit the desk with his fist, calmly but firmly.

"What do you want to know exactly, Mr. Private Eye?" he asked.

"This girl, she killed herself soon after she left the restaurant. So I'm just wondering about her emotional state when she was here."

"She was crying. Upset. That's all I remember," Martin replied.

The manager picked up Niral's card and read it.

"Who do you work for?"

"What do you mean?" Niral asked.

"I assume if you are a private eye, someone hired you."

"Her brother."

"Her brother who maybe yelled at her? Can I see your license?"

Niral gripped the chair. He sensed a few more bodies behind him.

46

"I don't have one. I work under another investigator."

The manager flipped the card at Niral, who caught it with his thighs.

"I think we're done answering questions, unless you can prove you have some official capacity here. Like a detective's badge. Otherwise, you can either sample our dining or leave."

"You don't have to be rude," Niral replied.

"You can go out the same way your boss did," the manager said.

19

Two big guys took him up by the shoulders, but Niral yanked free. They followed him to the other door, where Martin pushed him out into a small alley. Across from him was a garage occupied by skinny, haggard men sitting on oil cans, one eating an apple, the other gritting his teeth and eyeing him hungrily.

Niral brushed himself off and, trying to ignore the snickers of the bouncers, stared off into the East River and the skyscrapers beyond it, watching another boat cruise across the water, imagining how Priya must have felt on that boat after her brother had confronted her.

Then Niral moved the other way, down the long, empty road filled with old cars and down the alley toward the Citibank building and the new Long Island City of gentrification and developments, then past that to the old one that still preserved the ghettos and the artists and the PIs and porn producers. He thought of how Amrat had stumbled down these streets after being thrown out in the same way, after seeing his sister with Vishal, knowing he could do nothing about this union he despised.

But why did he despise it so much? He opposed Vishal on philosophical grounds, but then wouldn't he have opposed his sister too, whose education he had been paying for?

Niral moved through the maze of streets among an industrial wasteland until he finally found the corner of the church building, the 7 train station and the graffiti building across from it. He checked his watch and realized it was 11:15. As expected, Lance was sitting in Tony's Diner, waving at Niral as he climbed the steps to the train.

Niral stopped, pondered, and backtracked, heading toward the diner.

"We're gonna make you part of the team yet," Lance said as Niral sat across from him. "I'm gonna order you the best burger in Queens."

"I don't eat meat," Niral replied, but Lance ignored him, winking at the middle-aged waitress who gave him sass back.

"Then we're going to Gigglies," Lance stated.

"I'm not going to a strip club with you."

"Tell me, man, when's the last time you even got laid?"

"It's not what I'm looking for," Niral replied, hesitating as he said it.

"That's what every guy's looking for. Certainly if they're working for me."

The meal arrived. Niral dipped a french fry in ketchup and took a bite. Lance laughed.

"Aren't you curious to see Cherry naked? I see the way you looked at her."

Niral thought for a while, twirling another fry around in the tiny paper cup.

"Actually, that is a possibility. Are you sure she's there?"

"I don't got her schedule, man," Lance said, putting his hands behind his head. "But I see her most nights."

20

Niral immediately regretted his decision as they headed down Queens Boulevard and approached Gigglies. His heart raced faster than he thought it could, faster than since he'd woken up in Chloe's shower.

Lance was joking as they got in line outside Gigglies, but all Niral could think about was running toward the Queensboro Plaza station.

He told Lance he had changed his mind.

"Come on, man, you came this far. Check it out!"

Niral paid the cover and drink charge and got a glow-in-the-dark wristband on his right arm. They headed inside and passed a couple of topless girls and another two in bikinis making the rounds with the customers, hoping to entice a lap dance.

Niral tried to look away but couldn't. Lance got a seat at the table across from two Hispanic guys wearing Knicks jerseys. They were standing and hollering at the stage, shouting, "You the best! You the best, girl!"

Sure enough, Lauren was dancing in a schoolgirl uniform.

An older white woman came over to their table carrying a pad and two bottles of water.

"Iceman," she said. "What're you looking for today?"

"You, sexy mama. But I'll take Candy."

"She's with a customer now, but she'll be out in a second. She's got the big boobies for you, all right."

"She's my lady, mama. Perfect secretary for a CEO."

"How about your friend? I've never seen him."

"He's got a thing for schoolgirl."

"She's a valuable commodity. You see the homeboys yelling."

"You gotta hold 'em back. This guy look like ordinary folk to you?" Lance said, motioning in Niral's direction.

She examined Niral. "You're right, he looks like royalty. I'll make sure he gets her after she comes off stage. But you gotta give her a chance to pick up her winnings and freshen up."

"No problem, mama."

Niral saw the special attention Cherry gave to the customers sitting at the stage. They stuck out dollars bills, and she'd scoop them up with her tiny talents, giving them a feel, a wink, and a thanks. He glanced away from her and saw a large blonde emerge from beyond a blue curtain and come straight for Lance.

"Big momma!" he yelled as he stood and opened his arms. She shoved him back down and, turning, plopped on his lap. He gripped her ass with one hand, hugged her with the other arm, and gave her a light peck on the cheek with his big lips.

"This the meal I need this time of night," he said.

Niral checked the stage and saw Lauren was no longer there. She'd left behind a single, crumbled bill. The black dancer following her kicked it to the side of the stage.

He felt a tap on his shoulder.

"I gotta go in, bro," Lance said. "Wait for the madam; she'll get you Cherry."

"It's okay," Niral replied. "I think I'll go."

But he didn't move.

"It's up to you," Lance said. "But hopefully I see you on the other side."

Lance got up and, with Candy leading him by the hand, made his way toward the blue curtain.

Meanwhile, Niral continued to sit there, crouched over, staring ahead at a black door in the distance, his heart beating fast. He felt his eardrums shaking and his chest contract. He drank the water, but it didn't change anything.

He heard a commotion in front of him and stood up. Through a portal formed between the Hispanic men, he saw the madam leading Lauren toward him. The Hispanic guys were trying to get to her, but the madam was holding them off with her arm. Then Niral noticed a couple of bouncers come over.

"What's so special about him, man?" one of them asked. "You think he went to Harvard or something?"

The madam and one of the bouncers blockaded them. Meanwhile, Lauren smiled coyly at him and slid a finger down his bare left wrist.

"I know you," she said softly.

"Iceman explained it to you?" the madam asked. "Twenty for a dance that's a song long. But you want special time with her, fifteen minutes in a private room, that's seventy-five."

"Come on, cowboy, let's party," Lauren said.

"I don't know," Niral responded.

"I'm giving you special access to her, sweetheart, cuz Iceman's a good customer," the madam said. "Why not put it on Iceman's tab?"

Lauren took his hand and led him toward the blue curtain. He hesitated at first, then followed, glancing briefly at the bouncers. One was smirking.

21

Still wearing her schoolgirl uniform, she led him through the main lap dance room filled with businessmen and hustlers lounging on cushy black chairs directly across from each other, watching their counterparts being ground on. Then he saw Lance with his legs apart, entranced by Candy's assets as she sat on his lap and caressed his face with her hands.

Past a red curtain, Lauren brought him into a smaller, brighter room. She turned and pushed him onto a large, red-cushioned sofa in front of a small water fountain shaped like Cupid.

She unbuttoned her shirt, revealing her small, bare tits.

"No time for bras when your boobies are non-existent," she stated.

Niral's mouth was dry and balls of warm sweat formed on his brow.

"You didn't think I remembered big words in this place, did you?"

She giggled and unsnapped her skirt. She waved it in Niral's face and threw it over her shoulder. Using her stiletto heel, she spread his legs and raised his penis through his pants. She climbed onto him, putting her arms around his neck and placing her mouth next to his ear.

"You can kiss them if you want," she purred. Then she reared her head and flipped her hair back, leaving only one strand caressing her nipple.

Niral's lips were inches away.

"I shouldn't," he whispered, but he felt tempted.

"What are you, gay or something?"

"No, religious."

Her expression changed. "I've heard *that* before."

"Really? From a white guy?"

"What do you think?"

"I don't know."

"You could just taste. You're paying for it."

"Why don't we talk instead?"

She rolled her eyes. "Fine. Shoot."

Niral closed his eyes and said nothing.

"Or I'll give you a lap dance," Lauren said. "Maybe that'll turn you on."

"I'd rather know what a Yale grad is doing working in a strip club," he asked, opening his eyes again.

"You'd be surprised what you would do to pay the rent."

"I know what you mean."

"Then you shouldn't judge."

"I'm not."

"You are."

Lauren shifted and raised her arms. Niral moved his head out of the way and closed his eyes again. But soon, he felt something next to his nostril.

Reflexively, he sniffed. Something shot up his nose. He covered his nostrils with his palms and coughed. When he glanced at Lauren, she was smiling.

"What was that?" he asked.

"Happy dust," she answered.

Grabbing her hips, he pushed her onto the floor. He heard her screech as he got up, then felt a hard kick against his leg as he marched toward the curtain.

As he entered the lap dance room, the madam confronted him.

"That's seventy-five, sir," she said. "And there's a tip too. Average is

54

fifty bucks."

"Fuck you," he responded, barely getting it out as he stormed past, breathing hard.

In the main room, Lance and Candy were chatting.

"Niral!" he heard Lance call out. He headed to the exit, but the bouncers emerged and blocked him.

He heard the madam shouting behind him. Suddenly, he felt light-headed. The room began to spin. He fell into the breasts of a blonde girl.

22

When he woke in dim darkness, he stared up at a high, fractured ceiling. His eyes were wet, his mouth dry, and when he focused a bit more, he noticed silver tubes and wires crisscrossing each other. A faint light shone to his right. He turned and saw a single spotlight clasped onto a low desk, aimed at a nude girl seated on the floor, her knees up, her hand stretched lightly over a canvas as she painted the arm of what appeared to be a seated, brown sanyasi wearing a yellow dhoti.

Niral realized he was naked too. He sat up and felt for the janoi draped over his chest. He couldn't locate it. He began to freak, then he heard Lauren's voice.

"It's on the floor," she whispered. "I balled it up for you."

He reached out, clamping his hand down on the wood floor, searching the cool panels until he felt the soft, cotton ball. He squeezed it, then lifted it up. Desperately, he tried to unravel it, attempting to put the three strings together, like only his father could do.

When he failed, he began crying.

"What's wrong?" she asked.

He didn't answer, just felt the pain and flashes of memory.

"Deja vu," he finally said.

"Last night was good. You remember it?"

"You gave me something," Niral said. "You always give us something."

She continued to paint the arm of the sanyasi. Niral coughed, then saw his clothes bundled next to the mattress.

"What time is it?" he asked as he put them on.

"It's late. But I don't really count the time. I like to paint all night. Makes me forget everything else, I guess."

Niral finished putting on his clothes and stuffed the balled janoi into his pocket. He stood up, then stumbled and almost fell.

He rose again, feeling dizzy and light-headed.

"You shouldn't go out," Lauren said. "You're still high. Sleep until the morning. I won't bother you."

"I didn't tell my parents I wasn't coming home," Niral said. "They'll be worried."

"What a good son," she replied.

"I'm trying to be."

"But you're not. And you don't care about the girl you just fucked. Just another white object for you."

"You tricked me."

"You are all the same," she said, shaking her head. "Vaishyas, Brahmins, now Kshatriyas. Next stop is a Sudra, if I can find one."

"What do you mean?" he asked, but then, noticing the painting again, he recognized the round face and fierce eyes.

"Amrat," he exclaimed.

She threw down the brush, got up, and approached him. It was too much. He yanked the door open and fled down the dark hallway to a barely lit staircase.

Glancing back, he noticed the skinny, nude figure dominate the distant doorway against the bare light. He descended the stairs in the hollow of red darkness, past a lit doorway occupied by a voluptuous nude and the black-shirted asshole who usually stood outside the graffiti building. Then outside

57

the heavy door, he fled through the smoking girls with their black kohl-covered eyes into the dawn's early light.

PART III

23

Niral awoke in his basement apartment, lying on his bed. Above him, he saw a uniformed figure, seated upright like a meditating guru. In his hands, he played with what Niral believed was a slinky, until he rubbed his eyes and realized it was his janoi.

The figure was his father.

"I worked for twenty years in a job because I believed it was my duty," his father said in Gujarati. "Wearing this uniform. Putting people in prison. Even though I had broken with duty and tradition myself in India by marrying a Brahmin girl, in a time when an intercaste love marriage could result in death at the hands of her brother or her father. Yet when I moved to America, I felt so alienated in this new land that I wanted to maintain our Hindu traditions at any cost, and I believed you would follow in my footsteps. That's why I was angry when you decided not to go to college but moved to Brooklyn instead. But I realize now I was wrong. A person's nature has nothing to do with their heritage, nor are they tied to their past except to the extent that they allow themselves to be enslaved by it. The Brotherhood has taught me that, which is why I am devoted to it now in my retirement. And you should absolve yourself of the shame you feel about your past, and your current sense of false duty too, which perhaps you feel you must have to redeem yourself and follow in my footsteps. We are not Kshatriyas any longer. We are brothers."

"Deddy, I don't know..."

"I smell a woman's scent on you, Niral!" he yelled. "There was blood emerging from your nose. I don't want to know anything that you've done but that you are safe. This job has brought you back down into the dregs of society. I still remember when you called me that day from that girl's apartment."

"It's nothing, Deddy."

His father stood, Niral's janoi outstretched in his hands. "I am placing this janoi upstairs in God's room. Get bathed, dressed, and come upstairs. Narendrakaka is arriving for Donation Night. You will meet him, and we will discuss this further."

His father marched upstairs. Niral wept and punished his bed with hard punches. Then after a period of quiet and mindless reflection, he rose, wearing only his boxers, and swept across the basement to the bathroom.

24

Upstairs in the kitchen, Niral's mother heated and flipped rotlis on the stove, her back to him, refusing to turn. Narendrakaka's wife, Kauntiaunti, was rolling dough on a board adjacent to his mother and didn't notice him glide by.

Past them, in the living room, Narendrakaka relaxed on the draped recliner. He stood and welcomed Niral as he entered. Niral bowed to him with hands clasped in prayer, but before he could descend to Narendrakaka's feet, Narendrakaka raised him up by the shoulders.

"My son," he proclaimed, piercing Niral's eyes with his gaze as he firmly grasped Niral's shoulders. Then he pulled Niral toward him and hugged him.

Niral closed his eyes, then opened them again and watched his father not two feet away on the loveseat, awkwardly staring at the floor. He had changed into a white kafni-pajama.

Narendrakaka released him and commanded Niral to sit. Niral complied, sitting on the three-seat sofa across from them.

"Priya's death has been stressful for all of us," Narendrakaka stated, resuming his position on the recliner. "For the entire Brotherhood. And your father tells me that it has been for you, too."

Niral's father still wouldn't look at Niral.

"Amrat insisted we investigate her death, and we knew Stanuncle through your father and through you," Narendrakaka continued. "But the police must be right. There is no way we can disprove science. And it is making everyone crazy, when really we should put this business to rest. She is cremated. We must only convince Amrat to throw her ashes into the river."

"What are you saying?" Niral asked.

"I've told Stanuncle," Niral's father finally said, "we are no longer interested in investigating Priya's death. It is making you weak, moving you away from our goal to make you one with God, to achieve the perfection of your consciousness."

"I am finding out a lot," Niral said. "I know I messed up, but I won't get involved again..."

"Forget it, Niral," his father said. "These are all distractions. I thought having you work for Stanuncle would make you responsible, but I realize I should have pushed you toward the true Brotherhood goal of equality of man and the freedom of your mind. Quit this job and meditate. If you live within your means, my pension and your mother's salary should suffice until you are old. Or if you truly want to work, complete your bachelor's degree and apply for the police department as a clerk. Not this."

Narendrakaka stood and planted himself next to Niral on the three-seat. He placed his arm around Niral's shoulder. "If you want to continue to work for Stanuncle, that is okay with me," he said. "But this case is not good. Vishal and Meetal have both told me that it is not good for you or Amrat."

Niral wasn't sure what to say. He should have known that those two would have spoken to their father. So many thoughts went through his mind. But after all that had happened in the past, he wanted to obey his own father.

"Niral," Narendrakaka said, "we will allow you to give a donation to the Brotherhood Fund. I know you have wanted to since you rejoined the Brotherhood. This will allow you to forget the past and dedicate yourself to a future without caste, class, or other prejudice."

Suddenly, Niral felt elated. The Brotherhood Fund financed all Brotherhood operations throughout the Northeastern US, and donations were reserved only for those truly dedicated to the Brotherhood's aims and who expected nothing in return. It wasn't something devotees deducted on their taxes or bragged about. No one but Narendrakaka knew how much anyone gave or how much was in the fund.

Niral happily stood. He hesitated briefly, then proceeded to the bedroom. It had been Niral's bedroom when he was younger. Now his parents had converted it to a room dedicated to God.

On a large desk were pictures of the trinity of Gods—Vishnu, Brahma, and Shiva, Operator, Generator, Destroyer, which formed the one God, Atman—and a garlanded portrait of Bhen in India, who had inspired the Brotherhood movement worldwide. She had been ailing in recent months, and her husband, Bhai, had started to take over operations. Narendrakaka, in addition to being a spokesperson for the Northeastern US chapter, also often had a direct ear to Bhen, having been a devotee in India and having begun the movement in the US. Bhen had allowed the organization to be loose and localized, but Bhai wanted the operations to be more centralized and hierarchical, entrusting other Brothers in Texas and California to initiate the transition, one that had already started to take place and would be official once Bhen passed away.

But at this moment, Niral didn't care about all that. He dropped to his knees and glued his palms together. Observing his janoi carefully lain out in front of the portraits, he began weeping tears of regret and shame. He prayed for salvation and hoped that he wouldn't repeat his mistakes. He thanked God for his second chance. He tried to block out all of the details of his investigation, of what he had learned, of his tryst with Lauren, and focus on a picture in his head of the Divine: in his case, of Brahma. But thoughts of Meetal and Lauren kept interfering, so finally he stood up, took a twenty-dollar bill out of his pocket, and placed it on the plate for donations.

When he emerged, Kauntiaunti was serving dinner in the kitchen to Narendrakaka and his father. Niral's mother continued her work rolling rotlis.

Niral joined the men. Kauntiaunti filled his styrofoam thali with shak, rotli, khaman, and patra and his bowl with rice and dal, not heeding his calls for less until he physically restrained her arm as she perched the ladle over his dish.

She laughed.

"You must gain weight for your wedding," she insisted, dumping the rice anyway.

"Meetal is a good girl," Narendrakaka noted. His father nodded in agreement.

"I am so glad, in this country, that we are beyond caste," he continued. "Even in Gujarat now intercaste marriages are more common."

"We're just friends," Niral stated.

"Young people are very strange in this country," Narendrakaka said. "I keep telling Vishal to get married. He did not even tell us about Priya. It is unfortunate. If we had been involved, if the Brotherhood community had rallied around them, maybe she would not have killed herself."

As Niral finished eating, he saw lights approach their driveway, meaning that the cavalry of Brotherhood devotees had arrived for donations.

He got up. After his shameful night, he wanted to avoid the other Brotherhood devotees and any questions about his investigation of Priya's death, which apparently was coming to an end. His father's stare informed him as much and that he should continue his penance in the basement.

He told Narendrakaka he was leaving.

"Niral," Narendrakaka said, rising to meet him. "Do me a favor. When you can, go visit Dilipuncle. Amrat tells me he has not gone back to work since Priya's passing. He sulks and prays all day. Comfort him, if you can."

25

The next morning, as he descended the stairs from the overhead train in Long Island City, Niral tried to call Meetal.

She didn't answer.

He avoided looking at the graffiti building or the porn girls.

He entered the church building.

As Niral came into the office, he saw Stan at his desk working on the bookkeeping, a sealed manila envelope next to him.

"My main man," he said. "You've arrived for your eulogy."

"My dad talked to you?"

"He's concerned. Says he doesn't want you to work for me anymore."

"He doesn't want me to work at all. Just to become a sanyasi, a spiritual man."

"As if that's possible in this country," Stan replied, shutting down the computer and picking up the envelope. "Your dad's got some funny ideas. But what can I say? I've basically wasted my life chasing petty crooks, cheating husbands, and ungrateful wives. Maybe I should envy you. But I'm certainly going to miss you. You've been a good second eye. I'm gonna miss riding around snapping pictures. I certainly could have used you last night."

"Those are the pics?"

"Yup. An interesting bunch," he said.

He opened the drawer opposite his desk and placed it inside Macaday's case file. Then he removed an envelope from another file, closed it, and locked the drawer.

"Mrs. Macaday came by yesterday to make sure you would do her bidding," Niral informed him.

"You don't have to concern yourself with that now," Stan responded, handing an envelope to Niral. "What I do need you to do, for your final assignment, is to give this check to your friend Amrat."

"He paid you already?"

"A down payment, just to show me he had the funds. Wish I could keep them, believe me, with the way things are going. But it's not right if we're dropping him."

When Niral removed the check from the envelope, he noticed it was for one thousand dollars. From Stan's personal account.

"Why not just mail it?" Niral asked.

"You've gotta tell him we're ending it. I figured since you're friends..."

"I found out a lot, Stan."

"Don't tell me. I don't want to know. Just write it in your memoirs."

26

Niral took a train and bus to the residential neighborhood of Floral Park in eastern Queens. He knocked on the door of a single-family house with a trapezoidal roof.

After waiting a minute, feeling the cool wind of dusk, a weak voice asked for identification. Niral responded that he was Prakashbhai's son.

When the door creaked open, Dilipuncle awkwardly peeked out. He wore only a yellow-stained, white wife beater and white pajamas. His face was gaunt, and his neck had become so skinny that Niral saw thick blue veins sticking out.

When Niral was a teenager, Dilipuncle often wore suits, talked incessantly about his accounting profession, and gossiped about Bollywood stars. His wife had pushed the Brotherhood onto his children and on him; he had only come to meetings because of her.

After his wife's death from cancer, Dilipuncle had embraced the Brotherhood wholeheartedly, giving up his pretensions of an extravagant life and placing his money on a down payment for this home. Before that, they had lived in a dingy railroad apartment in Sunnyside, one Niral remembered playing in as a young teen with Amrat and Priya while overhearing Dilipuncle and his wife arguing about money and the Brotherhood.

Dilipuncle invited him inside. Niral removed his shoes and prayed at Dilipuncle's feet. He patted Niral's head lightly and then glided, like a ghost, into the living room. He gestured for Niral to sit on the sofa, then planted himself perpendicular to Niral before he realized he hadn't offered him anything to drink.

He suggested lemon sherbet.

"It's okay, Dilipuncle," Niral said. "How is your health?"

"I've been dead inside since my Priya's death," he responded. "I stay inside and pray."

Niral noticed, peeking out from his wife beater, a browned janoi.

"Narendrakaka told me you haven't been to work?" Niral asked.

"What use is there, my son?" he replied. "God doesn't care about numbers. Before the Brotherhood, I used to count numbers all the time—at work, at home—and I regarded myself as superior, as a Brahmin. Then, under the Brotherhood, I still thought about numbers. I just forgot I was a Brahmin. Now I realize being a Brahmin is my only salvation."

"You must eat, Dilipuncle."

"Did the great Gurus eat when they climbed the Himalayas, fasting when they marched and meditating when they stopped? First, when my wife died, I thought my life was over. Then Amrat saved us by quitting Harvard, by moving back home, by working and learning a good trade so he could replace Kirti's earnings, help pay the mortgage, and provide for Priya's education and her upkeep. I thought our life had improved, but I was wrong. Even under the Brotherhood, we lived materialistically. Instead of outer greed, we turned to inner greed, for the purpose of providing for Priya's future. Now that my *dikri* is no more, I realize our purpose was false. The only salvation is prayer. For all our salvations."

As Niral pondered this, he heard the front door creak open.

Amrat entered the living room, wearing a blue dress shirt and navy blue pants.

"Niral," he stated, clearly surprised, "I did not expect you. Are you here

70

to visit my father or me?"

"Both," Niral answered.

27

Upstairs in Amrat's room, Niral watched Amrat change into a yellow dhoti. He looked similar to the portrait Lauren had drawn. On the floor of Amrat's closet, Niral saw Priya's urn and a Mac laptop.

"Do you always change into that after work?" Niral asked.

"I meditate every evening, yes. Would you care to join me?"

"I need to talk to you about something first."

Amrat closed the closet door and adjusted his dhoti around his waist.

"Okay, Niral, speak," he said.

Niral removed the folded check from his pocket and handed it to Amrat.

"What is this?" Amrat asked.

"We can't investigate Priya's murder anymore."

"Cannot or will not?"

"Will not," Niral said.

"This is your boss's decision?"

"Yes."

"Vishal did not influence it in any way?"

"How could he?"

Amrat laughed in the only way he could, with a deep cackle.

"You would be surprised. Are you sure I cannot change your mind?"

"It's not my mind you need to change. I don't even work for Stan anymore."

"Then you would be available as an independent contractor?"

"My father wants me to become a sanyasi."

Amrat nodded and grinned slightly.

"I agree with him. I respect your father immensely, as you know. But first you must redeem your past life of unadulterated pleasure and achieve your duty as a Kshatriya. That is the third stage of life. The last is salvation through moksha."

"You don't agree with my father about skipping that step?"

"He did not skip it himself. He worked for the police department. You will only arrive at moksha by first solving Priya's murder."

"Most of my evidence points to her killing herself because of you."

"Me?"

"You were jealous and smothering. You scared her at the restaurant."

"You believe I would harm my flesh and blood? Someone I had given up everything to raise?"

"I'm not saying you meant to break her."

"Niral, I had my reasons for being upset."

"The same reason you had to be at a fancy restaurant even though you've cooked your own meals since your mother died? My father told me."

"There is an explanation for that."

"What, that you followed Priya and Vishal to that restaurant? That you had been stalking them for months? Maybe you even went back to the apartment later..."

"No! That was the first time I saw them together. It was a shock. It was a devastation, for God's sake!"

Amrat covered his face. Niral heard muffled cries underneath his hands.

"You wanted her to jump out of that window, Amrat, to punish her for shaming you," Niral continued, "Or you pushed her. One way or another."

"I would never harm my Priya. I loved my Priya. It was Vishal. It was his revenge."

"Revenge for what?"

Amrat turned away.

"You will not believe me if I tell you."

"Try me. I'm willing to believe anything at this point."

He turned back. "I did a good deed. But I took something from him, and he will not forgive me for it."

"Does it have anything to do with a stripper? Because I'm not sure how you would know one, but she knows you."

Amrat's eyes widened. Then he stared down at his toes.

"You know, then. Perhaps enough."

"I'm confused, to say the least."

Slowly he descended onto the mat. Then he gestured for Niral to follow, tapping the space in front of him, insisting Niral sit across from him.

"I will tell you the story then, of a Rakshasa," he said. "Listen."

28

It started, Amrat said, when he realized that the Brotherhood way was not enough for humanity to be cleansed of its moral wickedness.

"It is a racist operation. Only Indians were being targeted to give up their selfish ways. Bhai had that rule. So, I decided to move forward—without the rest."

He took his message to the Manhattan streets, specifically the station on the East Side on 53rd Street, standing next to the water fountain from morning until evening, preaching to people to give up their prejudices, passing out fliers he had designed and printed himself. Most ignored him. Some laughed. Others shoved him. Still, he persevered, and a few people, mainly old white ladies with poodles and Prada handbags, spoke to him for twenty, thirty minutes, trying to glean from him the secrets of life, what they weren't getting from their yoga instructors or their spiritual advisors closer to home. It made him feel warm inside, even when they got the whole Hindu religion wrong, not knowing there was truly one God and many manifestations and personifications of that Being.

But as the day wore on, Amrat became hungry—he had decided to fast—and chilled—it was the end of September, after all, and even frequent breaks inside the train station didn't make his cheeks and fingers any warmer. Still, he perked up when some teenagers stopped by and discussed with him the value of meditation and giving up worldly desires and things. That was until one picked him up by his legs and threw him into the fountain, his pamphlets in tow.

As the teens fled, some passersby helped him out of the water. But Amrat was freezing, shivering and, seeing his work drenched in the opaque water, devastated. After his helpers left, he realized that his wallet was also missing, his money and metro card with it.

When he approached the people emerging from the train station, they fled from him, perhaps thinking him a drenched, wild-eyed madman. He did not receive any pity from the train operator or a nearby policeman either.

He crawled into a corner and, shivering still, weighed his options. Fairly desperate, he finally decided to trek twenty blocks down and east to the river to an old friend's apartment, someone he hadn't seen in many years but who he knew lived there, someone who, despite reservations about his character, he believed he could trust due to his Brotherhood affiliations.

The Brotherhood's Big Brother's son, Vishal Patel.

29

After the guard let him up, Amrat listened at Vishal's door and heard riotous laughter. And when the door opened, someone beautiful stood there, a brunette with pigtails. Yet behind her, Amrat observed the most appalling debauchery.

"Vishal told me to dry myself off in the bathroom," Amrat recounted, "and he would set me up with a girl. I was not sure if he was joking, but I stayed in the bathroom for many minutes—it felt like an hour—until Vishal knocked on the door and asked me to emerge. I didn't know what else to do, so I entered the room again and averted my eyes from the sight that was the very opposite of what I had been preaching. My heart sank at the animalistic exercises of human lust I observed happening on the floor, men and women unclothed and with no thought to propriety or decency, with Vishal watching and laughing; he was even encouraging his lackeys on. He offered me a drink. I declined, and then he offered me hors d'oeuvres, but even my physical hunger could not match my spiritual devastation.

"Immediately, I headed for the balcony and was confronted by that commercial sight of hypocritical majesty. I ignored it and stared down at the abyss. And I felt, for a second, that my destiny lay there."

"You wanted to kill yourself?"

"It was too much to bear. The air was cold. I observed nothingness in the distance, that erection of civilization's discontent. But then she arrived. She grabbed my shoulders. She stopped me from leaping."

"Lauren?"

"She comforted me. She told me everything would be okay. And when she sensed my hunger and discomfort, she asked Vishal if she could take me out to eat. And he laughed at that, in his typical way, like he did when we were teenagers, always superior, like he was always one step ahead.

"That was the first time I had gone to a restaurant since my days at Harvard, when my mother's death had made me see the error of my godless ways. But I somehow felt special and comforted on that ride across the water, where Ganga resides, Lauren's blanket around me. And we landed at this shining institution where I was offered immaculate food.

"I broke my vows as my physical hunger overpowered me. Afterwards, I felt devastated again, remembering the experience of the night. Yet across from me, my salvation sat, hungry herself but not for food, for something else and eager to feast from my mind. That is when it started. That is when I realized that my true path lay not in educating thousands but in lifting up one individual at a time."

30

So Amrat came to Lauren's studio in Long Island City and taught her the Vedic ways, as she sat across from him like Niral was now. He taught her the four castes, the four roles of life, the four stages, the ways one should balance striving for material things with meditation and godly pursuits. And she eagerly absorbed her teacher's musings, weeping after every session with what she claimed were tears of joy.

She told Amrat she was desperately unhappy because she was forced to work at a strip club and at Vishal's orgies for his coworkers to pay the rent and be able to pursue her dream of art. She even thought of making porn like the smoking girls outside the graffiti building. The black-shirted producer had certainly made attempts to persuade her, but she was dead set against her parents ever having a chance to see the way she made a living in the city of dreams.

Amrat was torn. His heart broke as he listened to the way she was treated. He had some money saved up, but he had set it aside for Priya, his darling sister's education, and for his family if anything happened to him. It would be a betrayal if he ever used it for another purpose.

He tried to persuade her to become a secretary or find some other line of work. She said she had applied and no one was hiring. Anyway, it would never come close to what she made stripping and still give her time for her painting. She told Amrat the only thing that made her life worth living were his visits: he taught her and filled her life with the hope of spirituality and humanity.

Often, he would visit Gigglies at night and stand outside the club, staring at the men who entered, cringing at their laughter, internally crushed when he thought of the degrading things she did to survive. And he would pace along Queens Boulevard and wonder about the other lonely and debased souls that cruised the streets like phantoms gliding toward the release of death.

He grew to hate Vishal. He pondered how he could be so greedy and such a hypocrite; to be both Narendrakaka's son and yet still partake in such bacchanalia; to hire women to entertain his friends in such a sick and criminal manner, and yet refuse, with all the wealth he had accumulated, to help Lauren, choosing to exploit her instead.

But Lauren told him that Vishal knew about her meetings with Amrat. On the surface, Vishal made light of the situation, but she believed, based on some offhand comments, that he was jealous too. Amrat suspected this was because he was helping to expand Lauren's conception of the world. And that meant, eventually, she would have the mental will and clarity to release herself from Vishal's grasp.

One evening, only a couple of weeks after they met, Amrat told Lauren the first part of her lessons was over. Traditionally, in the ancient days of ashrams, students gave their teachers a present, a *guru dakshina*, whatever their instructors desired.

"Wow, this is the first thing you've ever asked for," she said.

"So you will give me anything?" Amrat asked.

Excitedly, she nodded.

He asked her to stop stripping.

Her lips quivered and whitened. She said she couldn't.

"I don't know what else to do," she replied, her body shaking.

"Fine. Then I will ask for something else," Amrat said. "But you must say yes."

"Okay," Lauren replied, cautiously. "What is it?"

"Don't work for Vishal anymore. Don't see him anymore."

This time, she couldn't refuse.

The next phase was fraught. As winter came, snow fell, and Amrat could only stop in Long Island City once in a while to see Lauren. Still, he felt Lauren's development and understanding of the nature of reality was improving. And Lauren would yearn for his visits more and more.

By the time Amrat felt the next phase of Lauren's education was over—that Lauren had learned the proper prayers by heart and, even more importantly, had absorbed them—it was already the end of March. By this time, she had learned to accept her parents and had called them in Maine and told them she existed.

Before, they had not known what had become of her. She had moved straight to New York after graduating from Yale, determined to pursue her dreams, and had told them not to contact her. They had been angry that she had passed on law school, and she did not want to hear more from them. Even now, as she reconnected with them, she hid her extracurricular activities from them. But she had embraced the idea of honoring and respecting her parents, a basic value, Amrat admitted, even he had forgotten as an arrogant youth before his mother's passing.

When the day arrived for Amrat's *guru dakshina* for the second phase, Lauren asked if she could give him a surprise present instead of catering to his demand.

This was not typical in regards to the ancient traditions, but reluctantly, Amrat said yes. She told him to come the next night, dressed well in western clothes, and she would give it to him. He already had an idea of what it would be, but he didn't want to speculate the root of so much unhappiness with unwarranted expectations.

When he opened the door to her studio, he was confronted at once with a portrait of himself, seated butterfly-style, dressed in a yellow dhoti. He laughed, both delighted and embarrassed at the depiction, and he was glad she had used her artistry for good. Before that, she had painted primarily grotesque images, mainly of the men who ogled her in clubs and parties. Now she had moved from the real and ugly to an ideal portrait of her hero, her teacher.

But what came next surprised and startled Amrat. For Lauren herself emerged from behind the portrait, stripped of clothing.

"Guru," she said, "please accept me."

She moved toward him. But he stepped back and crossed his arms.

"No, Lauren," he said. "That is wrong."

"Why?" Lauren asked. "Don't you find me attractive?"

"I swore celibacy when my mother died," he said. "I devoted myself to God's work and to my family."

"But I love you. I don't love those men in the club, but I love you."

She embraced him, even kissed him. He felt weak, but he pushed her away.

"You can show your love in another way, Lauren," he said. "It does not have to be the way of the flesh."

With that, she fled inside a small wash room. He could hear her weeping, then vomiting. Amrat fell on his knees and prayed to Shiva to help her through the crisis, to let her see the light. And twenty minutes later, she did emerge, in bra and panties, and sank down on her knees in front of him.

"Please forgive me, guru," she said. "I couldn't help it."

"Don't ask forgiveness of me," he replied, placing his hand on her head. "I know it is natural. But you must control your desires of the flesh. Only then can you hope to move on to the second phase of life, the path to earned success."

She rose and hugged him fiercely. Then, just as quickly, she unclasped herself, wiped her tears, and disappeared again. Amrat thanked God he hadn't fallen into the lustful fit felt by Pandu when he had seen his wife taking a bath in the forest in the Mahabharata.

When she re-emerged, she wore a blue cocktail dress.

"There's another reason I asked you to wear those clothes," she said. "I wanted to take you out to eat."

"I do not eat outside food," he replied. "That was once only—for a special circumstance."

"This circumstance is special," she insisted, taking his hand and leading him out.

They strolled hand-in-hand through the streets of Long Island City, both gentrified and ghetto, until they approached the water and the back entrance of The Dock. Two bouncers allowed them in, but they were told, given the influx of customers from Manhattan, that they would have to wait half an hour. Amrat wanted to leave, but Lauren insisted they persevere, excited to dine with her guru. And luckily, only five minutes later, they were told to follow a waiter to their table.

When Amrat saw Priya and Vishal together, he told Niral he felt like his heart had exploded within his chest. Forgetting about Lauren's presence, he had approached them.

"I just asked her why," Amrat recalled. "She looked at me like her world had exploded too. And do you know what he did? He laughed. In that same superior way. That is when I knew. He had manipulated my Priya for my taking Lauren from him. And murdering her was the final nail in the coffin of his revenge."

"So you scared her," Niral concluded. "She realized her secret was out; her days were numbered; her brother would never forgive her."

"I would never hurt my Priya."

"Would Vishal murder his girlfriend just because you told Lauren to stop seeing him?"

"Think about how dastardly his feat was. To seek her out, to make her believe that she was in love. Perhaps he even calculated Lauren's taking me to the restaurant..."

"All conjecture. Wild conjecture."

"You know Vishal's character. Even when we were children."

"Ambitious, manipulative, at times. But a murderer?"

"If he would hire women to sleep with his friends at parties..."

"I can't believe that's true," Niral said.

"You're thinking they would not have to be paid, given your past?"

"Frankly, yes."

"Vishal has money. He has achieved success from nothing. Now his next goal should be duty."

"He says it is."

"But really, it is power. And petty revenge."

"Can you prove it?"

"Through you, Niral, I will. Help me prove it."

"I am supposed to become a sanyasi."

"You will see that you will not be able to achieve it without this step."

"What happened to Lauren?"

"She fled. Outraged by my behavior, perhaps. I have not seen her or spoken to her since. You see, Niral, I must redeem myself too."

PART IV

36

Outside the building that headquartered LedaCorp, Niral was double-parked in his father's car, hoping a cop wouldn't spot him. During the day, his father would visit other Indians' homes, trying to convince them of the superiority of Brotherhood ways, sometimes taking his own car, other times another uncle's.

Today was the latter situation, and Niral figured it was as good a time as any to borrow the old man's vehicle for some investigative work. One cop had already stopped by to question him, but when Niral had shown him his father's old police permit, the Blue Code had shielded him. But he wasn't confident about a second time, so he hoped Vishal would be swift.

Finally, as the sun began to descend against the Statue of Liberty in the far distance, Vishal emerged from the building and got into the waiting limo. Niral tailed the vehicle up FDR Drive, out into Midtown, then northeast over to the low 50s in Midtown East.

Vishal's chauffeur double-parked in front of a restaurant. Vishal left the limo and entered the establishment.

A few cars behind, Niral took out a rented camera Amrat had paid for and positioned the camera's long lens like Stan had taught him, waiting patiently. An hour later, Vishal emerged with another man in a suit.

Niral recognized him. He had never seen him in person, but the face in the zoom matched a photo Niral remembered of Mr. Macaday, the alleged cheating husband from Forest Hill.

The coincidence startled Niral. He couldn't figure out the connection, but frantically, he began taking pictures.

37

The next morning, Niral rose, performing his morning prayer while staring at his palms. Then he took a shower and, donning a kafni pajama, sat butterfly-style and meditated, concentrating as well as he could on an image of Brahma, the Generator of the world. When he finished, he uploaded the pictures from the day before on his computer, then dialed Detective Savard, who picked up right away.

"Definitely her blood," he confirmed. "And we have someone else's DNA on it too. Not her roommate's; we ruled that out. But it doesn't match anyone in the criminal database."

"What's the next step?"

"We can't compel anyone to give DNA, and it might not be our best angle anyway. So we've got to get it through deceit. A cup, cigarette, something. I can meet with some people close to her as a second interview. See if they'll give it up over coffee."

"What if I got it? Would it be legit?"

"You're not even an official PI, let alone a cop. And you knew her, and you found the scarf. So it might not go over well, but we can see how the DA could spin it. Still, the DNA could have nothing to do with the murder or suicide. Remember, you discovered it downstairs. Someone could have taken it from the body after it landed. Actually, that would explain the blood better than somebody taking it when they pushed her."

"Weren't there people watching the body after it landed?"

"I'm just saying, it's possible. We've gotta cover all bases. And I'll see if we can get another look at the autopsy files of the ME. See if anything we missed indicates trauma before the fall. If she hadn't been cremated, we could do a second autopsy."

"Yeah," Niral said under his breath. "Hindu culture."

After hanging up, Niral examined the photos taken the day before, churning his mind, trying to figure out how Vishal and Mr. Macaday knew each other. He knew Mr. Macaday was a retired investment banker, lucky for him, since all the i-banks had failed in the 2008 collapse. Nowadays, he just sat on boards and invested his money. Odds were Mr. Macaday was one of Vishal's investors. But he couldn't know for sure without seeing Vishal's files or asking him.

Maybe it was a coincidence that they knew each other, or maybe not. He could ask Stan if he'd encountered Vishal in his surveillance of Mr. Macaday, but he needed to find a way to do so without revealing his continuing investigation into Priya's death. Niral didn't want Stan tipping off Niral's father.

38

Niral returned to the scene of the crime and interviewed Priya's hallmates. A couple said they'd woken up. It could have been from a scream or a thud, but they weren't sure, and they'd gone back to sleep until the police had arrived at their doors. The death had occurred late at night, around four a.m., when even college kids were asleep and the dorm was quiet. None of them said they really knew Priya because she and Jody were older.

Then, he visited the apartment building across the street and interviewed people there about whether they had seen anything, but again, he got the same reply: even in the city that never sleeps, people slept. One lady said she'd heard a thud, but she had gone back to sleep and only woke up when she heard cop sirens. Nobody had been staring out the window, waiting to spy on a struggle across the way.

But Niral did run into a familiar person as he left the building and headed toward the subway. She no longer had a nose ring like a bull, and her short hair wasn't colored partially purple any longer, but she still retained that sly glance and that slick smile with the probing eyes.

"If it isn't Niral the Viral Infection," Chloe said.

Niral didn't respond.

"You don't remember me or something?"

"Without the nose ring? It's hard."

She laughed. "You were always the witty one. Look at you. You've changed, I think, since the last time I laid eyes."

"How so?"

"Just the way you carry yourself, maybe. Like a grown-up. You're old enough, anyway. I don't know what you were doing hanging out with us."

"Me neither. How's Jeremy?"

"Haven't seen him. I think he moved to Texas or something, to do Teach for America. It's crazy how people can get all altruistic all of a sudden."

"Bye, Chloe," Niral said, but after he walked a few steps, he glanced back.

"Can't stay away for long," she chided him. "You'll be back, baby. I'm still in the same place, and I still lick lollipops. Come visit sometime."

39

"It's true," Vishal admitted, putting down his cup, "she came to my parties, but I didn't pay her. What kind of a guy do you think I am?"

He and Niral were having samosas and tea inside a Dosa Hut in Flushing. Juan was outside, minding the limo.

"Just something Amrat mentioned when I talked to him. I was curious."

"You've gotta let it go, man," Vishal said. "My dad told me you're off trying to be some kind of guru. Forget about the past and join my crew. You can come to all the parties you want."

"I'm not—"

"Interested, I know. You're trying to get away from all that sex shit. My coworkers do what they want. I was monogamous with Priya. Never had any of it. But it was all consensual, legit, and it's not like I advertised it as a sex party. True, when people have money, it can get to their heads and their balls. But you don't have to be a part of it. Which also brings me back to Meetal..."

"She walked out on me."

"I talked to her about that. She thought you were trying to probe. I explained you were overzealous because of Priya. Now you're fine. She's willing to see you again."

"I don't know."

"Don't worry. One time thing. She's into guys trying to redeem themselves. That's sexy to a writer, as you know." Vishal dripped some chutney onto the samosa with a spoon, first brown then green.

"I like mixing it, for that extra zing. God, it's been years since I've been in a Dosa Hut."

"You should try the Pondicherry Dosa here."

"Spicy. I need to go back to India too, visit the south. I've never been. I hear people are nicer there than in Gujarat."

"My mom says Modi has done wonders," Niral said.

"Some say he's a dictator, some a God." He consumed the crust of his last samosa and licked his fingers. "Listen, I'm busy today, but why don't you come down to LedaCorp tomorrow? I'll show you around a bit, you can get a feel, and maybe we can slide you in."

"My dad will love that."

"We won't tell him at first. He's always on his missionary trips, so he won't catch on," Vishal said. "I'd go too, but I give back in other ways, of course."

"Of course."

"You'd be surprised about our folks. My dad claims he's given up material things; he's still living in that shit apartment above the deli in Jackson Heights. But let me tell you something: when we go to weddings, he always shows me off as his fucking rich-ass hedge fund son who gives millions to the Brotherhood Fund. Believe me, they're all like that on the inside."

He dropped the cup off at the precinct, wrapped in a plastic Ziploc bag.

"You didn't touch it yourself, did you?" Savard asked.

Niral held up his hands.

"Chopsticks. After he left."

"I'll have the lab examine it. And I've got something for you."

He ruffled through the papers on his desk and lifted up a folder.

"ME re-examined the report. Turns out they missed a gash on her neck that might not be from the fall. Could be somebody grabbed her shawl as she was falling out the window, and based on her velocity, he could have cut her deep, maybe even spun her around. And because they were leaning out, could be why we didn't find any blood splatter or DNA inside."

"Are you sure?"

"It's a theory but a good possibility. Makes it possible the killer dumped it as he left the building. Makes it possible there was a killer."

"Enough to reopen the case?"

"It's not already?" Savard said, knocking twice on the desk.

Niral was so happy, he got off the subway at Jackson Heights and ran to the deli. Meetal was working behind the counter, scooping up change for a white guy buying a newspaper.

"I didn't expect to see you," Meetal blurted out, smiling at him. Niral had the urge to tell her about the case but held his tongue at the last minute. Narendrakaka came out of the back as the white guy left the store after giving Niral a dirty look.

"Niral, so good to see you," Narendrakaka said.

"It's been a long time since I've been here," Niral responded. "It still has the smell of betel nuts."

"And the sight of porn magazines," Meetal added.

"Meetal," Narendrakaka said.

"It's true."

"We are not here to judge the tastes of others."

"Yes, Pappa."

Niral paced to the back of the store, felt the coolness of the fridge, then circled around the shelves of potato chips and returned to the front.

"Looks good, like I remembered it."

"Such a fun spring break for me," Meetal said.

"It is quiet," Narendrakaka stated. "Meetal, why don't you show Niral our apartment?"

"He's been there before."

"It's been years," Niral said. "But are you sure you're okay with that,

Narendrakaka?"

"You are not fifteen anymore, Niral," he responded. "Let Meetal show you our apartment."

They climbed up the stairs. The apartment door hadn't even closed when Meetal turned and pinned him against the wall. She held his face close, not allowing him to escape until they had tasted each other's tongues.

He put his hands on her hips and started moving them up her body, but as they slid toward her breasts, she stopped them and led them back down to her hips. She pulled her lips away.

"I'm sorry I was a bitch," she said.

"It's okay. I shouldn't have pried."

They kissed again. She pulled him toward the sofa, and they crashed down on it. He devoured her neck until she pushed him away again.

"God, this feels so wrong," she said, panting.

"Like you're kissing your brother?" he asked.

"Don't be disgusting," she replied, hitting his chest, but he laughed, and then they went at it again.

Afterwards, sitting on the floor, he leaned against the sofa. Her head was on his lap as she lay down, knees bent, staring up at the ceiling. He played with her hair.

"Vishal told me you might start working for him," Meetal said.

"It's a possibility."

"Normally, I would say don't do it."

"Why? He's your brother, right?"

"I guess I used to think it was evil. My dad doesn't approve. But now I realize this is the real world. We need to pay bills."

"There are some more important things than paying bills."

"Nothing's more important on a basic level."

"What are you implying?"

"What do you mean?"

"About us?"

She didn't say anything at first, just played with her own hair, while he rubbed her stomach under her shirt and buried his finger in her warm belly button.

"I'm just here for the break," she finally said. "And the dance. But I'll be back in a couple of months for good. Maybe you'll be set up with my brother by then."

"Your dad's pushing it?"

"Everyone's pushing it, Niral. And why not? You don't have a white girl on the side, do you?"

"No," he replied.

"I've dated my share of douchebags. But that's over. We've gotta get real now. I sent out a gadzillion job applications and got nothing back. I realize I was an idiot to get that stupid degree."

"We're all idiots," he said.

44

The elevator was broken, and the walk-up to the apartment in Alphabet City had crooked wooden steps sprayed with graffiti spelling out anti-government slogans. Yet when Niral entered the couple's apartment, he found himself enveloped in a pristine little studio where the windows were ornamented with fresh lilacs and daisies and the smell of all-natural, strawberry-scented air freshener permeated his nostrils.

"It's just like we told the cops," the boyfriend explained, lying sideways on his hammock chair. "We were strolling back from the park, just minding our own business, when this object just plops down on the sidewalk."

His girlfriend, sitting in the kitchen, closed her eyes and covered her ears.

"She doesn't want to remember," he said. "I wish you hadn't come, man. It's reliving bad memories."

"Did you actually see her fall?"

"No way. Like I said, we heard the plop, like a soup dumpling crashing on the floor, man. And then we saw her. I had to grab my girl's arm to keep her from running away, and I put my hand over her mouth to keep her from screaming."

"You didn't look up at all to see where she had come from?"

"Honestly, I don't remember."

"Maybe she does."

"I prefer you don't ask her."

Niral considered her for a second. Then, he walked over.

"You remember seeing anyone in the window, ma'am? Maybe you saw her fall?"

Her boyfriend stood up and approached Niral. He was much taller, over six feet, and his ears were studded all the way down.

"I think you should leave us alone now."

"You don't care?"

"We told you what we know. We already got cited for being in the park too late. We don't need any more trouble."

"There was a man," the old woman said, dropping her spoon into her bowl. "He had the look of a spook, staring down from the window, like Amadeus admiring his magnum opus."

"Don't listen to her," the man beside her said, "she makes things up all the time."

"Do you remember what he looked like?" Niral asked, gazing around the soup kitchen, making sure no one else was taking a special interest.

"A skinny man. A mad man."

"Can you be more specific?"

"You're wasting your time," the man insisted. "She's nuts. One time, she laid outside the Brooklyn Academy all winter, thinking she could regain her musical powers from when she was younger. Everyone looks like fucking Mozart to her."

"He was a maestro," she said. "He was a designer."

"Why didn't you tell the police this?"

"The student never tells," she said. "She never reveals her master's secrets. Especially when the master has a present for her."

"What present?"

"A scarf. He's dangling it around. It's got jewels on it. Just for her pleasure."

In the morning, Niral performed his prayers dressed in his kafni-pajama. Once his father left, he put on a suit, the only one in his closet. It was a blue suit his father had bought for him from India, hoping one day he would return to his homeland in it. It had that special Indian feel and embroidery, alien to America. But Niral had no other choice.

He took the subway into Manhattan, passing Amrat's old apartment in Sunnyside, then the Long Island City digs: the graffiti building, the church, Tony's Diner. He switched at Grand Central to a downtown train.

Outside LedaCorp, he quickly consumed a bagel with cream cheese. Vishal's secretary had him wait, so he tried to read the Financial Times while his future coworkers filed in, making guy-talk about women they'd seen in the street and on the elevator. One, a balding man with brown hair who nevertheless didn't look above twenty-five, did a double-take as he evaluated Niral's suit, elbowing some of the others as they shuffled by and shared in his amusement.

Finally, Vishal emerged from his office in a pristine Brooks Brothers outfit. He took in Niral's attire.

"Unique," Vishal said. "Going back to the old days. I'll spruce you up, don't worry."

He put his arm around Niral and led him into the room.

"Everyone," he announced, "this is the new guy. Don't haze him too much. He's a childhood friend of mine. In fact, Justin," he ordered, pointing to the balding man, "I want you to show him the ropes. You'll start with derivatives, Niral. Fun stuff. Report back to me after lunch."

Justin forced a smile as Niral came over to him and shook his hand.

"You from India? I love India," he said.

"No. I was born here."

He checked out Niral's suit again, pursed his lips, and nodded.

He had Niral sit by him as he traded on his computer, explaining to him the symbols of companies, the figures, how and when to make trades and when to hold off, etc. Niral felt it was too much information for him to absorb in one morning, but he still tried to understand as the other workers shouted above him, sometimes in triumph, other times in dismay or horror.

Before Niral knew it, Vishal's secretary was standing next to him, ordering him to Vishal's office.

"How do you feel?" Vishal asked, eating a sandwich.

"Overwhelmed," Niral replied.

"Not so glam-glam, is it? I told you, this isn't the fun part. But once you get the hang of it, you'll start making the dough. It'll take a while. But we've got time, don't we?"

47

After work, Niral took the bus out to Dilipuncle's house, hoping he could get Amrat's DNA, too. When he arrived, he found the door open and the living room lights on. He called out. No one responded.

As he passed the living room and approached the stairs to the second floor, he noticed the door ajar in one of the two bedrooms. When he peeked inside, he saw Dilipuncle sitting palathi in front of a mandir, next to a king-sized bed, humming "Om-ma-om" softly, eyes closed, surrounded by pictures of Shiva and Laxmi.

Quietly, Niral climbed the stairs.

Amrat's room was empty. Niral immediately opened the drawers, but he found just Amrat's checkbook in which he had recorded the check to Stan and numerous monthly payments, including for Priya's tuition and the mortgage on the house. Oddly, the payments for the mortgage were to a company called Devi Incorporated, which wasn't a bank Niral had ever heard of.

Inside his closet, Niral found a laptop that he thought might be Priya's. He turned it on, saw Priya's name in the account portion, and began to peruse.

He did a finder search for Vishal's name, but only found one file mentioning him. It was a letter from Priya to her father, dated January, in which she asked him to send her money because Amrat's portion wasn't enough and she needed to go shopping for some amazing saris in Jackson Heights that, while searching the net, she'd noticed were straight from a new, dynamic factory in Surat. She mentioned that Vishal wasn't giving her anything extra either and that she trusted her father would have it because Amrat gave him what was left over. Niral didn't understand what that meant, but it seemed to imply that Dilipuncle had known about Vishal and Priya's relationship, even though Amrat hadn't.

He emailed the letter to himself, then checked for anything else that was incriminating. He located just a series of letters to Amrat, apparently copies of emails she had saved into Word, where she asked him to come over to fix things in her apartment. But no letters to Vishal himself. For some reason, if she had contacted him, she didn't leave a trace on her hard drive.

Niral emailed Amrat's letters to himself, then shut down the computer, put it back into the closet, made sure everything was like it was when he had entered, and returned to the first floor.

When he checked Dilipuncle's room again, he wasn't there. So Niral let himself in. Again, he opened drawers and found Dilipuncle's checkbooks too.

One was labeled "Devi Incorporated." When Niral looked through it, he found the account only had checks deposited from Amrat and payments made to Priya.

Suddenly, he heard a noise outside the door. He turned and saw Dilipuncle staring into the room with a blank expression on his face.

He stumbled inside. Niral smelled alcohol on his breath as Dilipuncle approached. He dropped the checkbooks into the drawer and shut it with his butt.

Then, Dilipuncle, cursing, fell over on him.

Niral poured Dilipuncle a few glasses of water from a pitcher as they sat together in his living room, Niral blowing a fan on Dilipuncle's face to keep him awake.

Once he was sober enough, Niral turned off the fan and asked Dilipuncle about the checkbook.

"I'm sorry about my drinking, Niral," Dilipuncle said, rubbing his head and slurring his words slightly. "Along with God, I only have the bottle and the occasional woman. Nothing else."

"Dilipuncle. Why do you have the checkbook for the mortgage company?" Niral asked.

Dilipuncle drank some water and shook his head. "I am sorry you have to find out this way, Niral. I must admit, we have owned this house since Kirti died."

"Owned the house?" Niral asked. "And Amrat didn't know? You were stealing money from him?"

"You must understand, Niral, Amrat does not think like a normal person. He believes only the essential aspects of life are necessary. He does not understand the material things must be enjoyed, too, sometimes. He was intent on paying for as much as possible, so we let him. But Priya and I, we understood that he would never give us anything for the extra things that make life worth living outside of God. So we fooled him, but we did not do it for a bad reason. We were not bad people. He felt he was helping the family, and he would have never used the money himself, so there was no harm. He always seemed satisfied when he gave me the check, so who was I to break his satisfaction?"

"What about your earnings?" Niral asked.

"We have bills Amrat did not pay for," he replied.

"And you knew about Vishal and Priya?"

"Priya and I were close. She told me she was dating him but asked me not to tell anyone. So I did not."

"If Amrat found out you were scamming him, he would have been angry at Priya, too, right?"

Dilipuncle raised his finger in warning.

"Amrat does not know, even now. He has never said anything. But even so, he would never harm Priya. Do not even think it."

50

The next day Niral returned to LedaCorp, this time wearing a different shirt and without a tie.

"Remind me to take you shopping," Vishal said.

Justin was nervous that morning. He'd staked a lot of his portfolio on a Hong Kong company that suddenly was tanking.

"Asia's not supposed to sink," Justin said.

"Hedge it," another associate advised, but Justin said he'd let it ride.

"It's still morning. Could come up by afternoon. Just got too much on it."

"Sell a few shares and put it in oil futures. Then hedge the rest."

Justin wouldn't budge. "I've got too much confidence in it."

"Never good to have all your eggs in one basket."

"Not all. Just a lot."

When Niral went back to Vishal's office during lunch time, he admitted some of it was exciting.

"Ups and downs, baby," Vishal said.

"It's unnerving. I guess that's what makes it exciting. Kind of like art."

"But in art, you can never win."

"And you never even feel fulfilled."

"Here, at least you feel good on the outside. I'll show you what I mean, eventually. Just like Carty showed me. But right now, I've got a subordinate to take out to lunch."

"Justin?"

"I'm a little concerned about his portfolio. Figured we could examine it over some gnocchi. Coming?"

"Mind if I check my email?"

"Special girl in your life, huh? Of course. Knock yourself out."

51

As soon as Vishal was out of sight, Niral was at his computer. Immediately, he did a search for "Macaday."

A few files came up. He opened a couple. They were pdfs listing investors and assets. No question that Macaday had a large stake in LedaCorp.

Next was an Excel spreadsheet and then a Quickbooks file listing money coming in and out of the fund. Niral found these a bit more decipherable because they were similar to the Quickbooks reports he did for Stan.

As he scrolled down, he saw a number of payments to the Brotherhood Fund, mostly in the hundreds of thousands, and with one large payment of nearly one million dollars in October.

Niral cringed in jealousy at the amount. Then, a few moments later, he hit the jackpot. He came across a familiar name: Tim McNally, the priest in charge of the church building that housed Lorenzo Investigations. It was on a check that hadn't been sent out yet, and the amount wasn't filled in either.

The last file Niral opened was a large PDF. Different than the others, it included maps as well as assets and investors. The graphs seemed to depict the area of Long Island City that included the church building, Tony's Diner, and the graffiti building. It began around the area where The Dock was located and ended at Queensboro Plaza, including Gigglies.

Niral was so engrossed in the presentation that he barely heard a knock on the glass. When he looked up, he saw some of the guys peeking in through the shades, drinking coffee, and waving at him. He smiled and waved back, then quickly opened his email account. He attached all the files as he saw Vishal approaching the window with Justin. He sent the email, then quickly logged out and shut the browser.

Vishal came inside and shut the door.

"You've gotta keep them happy. Keep them hungry. Not too much weight, not too much hand-holding. Just right. Probably the only thing Carty taught me that was worth a damn."

Niral smiled, then realized, out of the corner of his eye, that the files were still open.

"Emailing Meetal?" Vishal asked. "She told me you guys had patched things up."

"Yeah," he answered, "just finishing things up."

"Can I be a nosy brother and peek?"

"That's okay," Niral said, closing the files. "I'd rather not get too incestuous."

Vishal laughed, leaning on one of his tables.

"When you're family, it'll be hard not to be close."

52

Back home, Niral downloaded the files onto his computer and examined them. The Long Island City development project didn't seem to be LedaCorp's. Instead, another firm entitled Coleman Investments was the titleholder. Apparently, the plan was to buy up all the property in that general area, get approval from the community board, demolish the site, and then build a range of entertainment complexes, from malls and massive movie theaters to an amusement park, OTBs, and high-end strip clubs catering to wealthy clientele.

Coleman Investments' current holdings included The Dock, Gigglies, the graffiti building, and a few housing projects, small apartment complexes, and warehouses. The church building, Tony's Diner, and a few other restaurants and private establishments were the only places the firm didn't control, and Niral figured there must have been a large campaign to buy up the property. He read a couple of letters directed at the board to force the owners to sell, citing eminent domain, but at their meetings, the board had refused and even voted down proposals to build the site. Still, Coleman Investments seemed to have approval from the right places, and the votes were close, meaning even if eminent domain wasn't a factor now, eventually the board could cave. But rather than fight it out that way, a few letters back and forth from names like "Mr. Brown" and "Mr. Edmonds" specified that they preferred to quietly buy up the properties rather than make a big deal about the project in the press.

Vishal's LedaCorp was a stakeholder in the scheme, but it wasn't the only one. Mr. Macaday had also invested substantially. Yet most of the companies had funny names like Sheephard and Cheapdate, making Niral suspect they might have been shadow companies, fronts, or maybe the creations of some Wall Street whiz kid.

As he was trying to figure out Father McNally's involvement, Niral's father popped his head down and asked Niral to come up. Upstairs, he saw the other major Brotherhood uncles from other regions of the country in his living room: Sureshuncle, Alkeshuncle, and Premuncle.

He placed his palms together and bowed to Alkeshuncle, who gently padded him on the head, but then another pair of hands lifted him up. He stared into Narendrakaka's wet eyes, and when he scanned the room again, he noticed all the faces were dour. He heard light wailing through the shut door of God's room.

"Niral," Narendrakaka said, gripping his shoulders tightly, "we just heard. Bhen has passed away."

As Niral pondered this news, tearful devotees began arriving, and he heard Sureshuncle and Premuncle speaking to Narendrakaka in God's room.

"Narendra," Premuncle said, his hand on Narendrakaka's shoulder, "Bhai has already willed it. The Brotherhood will be centralized. Sureshuncle will be in charge of the North American operations. The Fund will be centralized too, for good. All donations will go directly to Ayodhya, and Bhai will decide how the funds will be distributed. Bhai will continue to forgive the transgressions of the past. But with your record, you cannot remain the Big Brother. Eventually, you will have to step down."

A few hours later, after Niral had collected himself, his parents descended to the basement and told Niral that for the next two weeks, the ladies would have a mourning period for Bhen. They would use the basement for their gatherings, so he would have to relocate to God's room. That meant taking his computer and papers upstairs, and his parents would be home often now, making it more difficult to sneak out. He felt bad for Bhen and Narendrakaka, but the move complicated things for him, as if they weren't complicated enough.

After he moved his stuff upstairs, he locked himself in God's room and prayed to the Trinity, and especially to Brahma, picturing him in his mind more clearly than ever. He felt the Generator was a greater part of him now, an aspect of his being, just one step closer to achieving the perfection of his consciousness and its oneness with Atman. He was sorry that Bhen's death had to coincide with this milestone, but he figured if every life began and ended and that the cycles of life included endless reincarnation until the soul reached oneness with the Supreme Being, then he should be glad that Bhen's soul had inspired so many while it was on earth.

When he called Meetal, she was crying.

"I didn't realize Bhen meant so much to you," he said.

"Are you kidding? I always held it in, but she did. She was an inspiration. She's what I held onto when I followed my dream into journalism school."

"And now?"

"My dad tells me they'll celebrate her life and achievements when I perform my dance on Holi. He says it will honor her, but I don't know how I'm going to live up to it, Niral. And then a couple of days later, I'll be gone for another couple of months."

"So I won't see you."

"We can talk on the phone."

"Yeah, long distance works great. I remember when my ex went back to Connecticut on her breaks..."

"You've got an ex?"

"You told me you had fifty."

"Not fifty. I didn't say that many." She laughed.

"Honestly, I don't want to talk about it."

"I understand. But why bring her up at all? You think that's fair to me?"

"You brought up yours before."

She paused. "That is true."

"Women," Niral said.

55

After he hung up, Amrat called him.

"You've heard the news."

"How do you feel?" Niral asked.

"Another being has passed into another life. What can be tragic about that? But things will be bad under Bhai. The Brotherhood will pass even further down an erroneous path."

"Of racism?"

"Of inclusion, exclusion. Collusion, I suspect. Throughout history, many movements have been ruined as the founder is deified and the successors use it for their own benefit. Look at Jesus, Mohammed—almost everyone else. You will see them putting up pictures of her everywhere now, proclaiming equality, when really there is none. Only the surface will show it, but underneath, the same divisions will remain and fester, the same prejudices and grievances, and new ones will develop, too. Do not be fooled, Niral. You may do your part, as you must, but do not be fooled."

"I think it's too early to be making predictions."

"I know you want so badly to believe, Niral, because it is your chance at redemption. But remember, action leads to redemption, not simple belief. What have you discovered about my lovely Priya?"

"I'm still working. It's developing."

"My father is still in a depressed state, always praying. Detective Savard came here and had some tea with me. He said he is reopening the case because of you, but he could not tell me anything. Can you?"

"I've got pieces. I'm still waiting on some things. I want to give you the whole picture when I have it."

"Okay, Niral," Amrat said with resignation. "I will trust you. I must."

Finally, Niral called Vishal.

"It's going to be difficult getting out of the house," Niral said.

"No problem. I've heard they've got you in God's room while the ladies do bhajans downstairs? It never ends."

"You don't mind?"

"Take a break. Absorb everything. Let me know when you can come back. There's no hurry. Hopefully Justin will be here to fill you in."

"Doesn't sound like you're upset about Bhen."

"People live and die. But I have to say, I'm more happy than sad. Now that my dad's out of the Brotherhood's administrative and financial shit, he can finally forget about the Brotherhood Fund and sell that stupid deli. I'll fly him and Mummy down to Florida. They'll retire like kings. He needed this jolt to see the light."

"Meetal and I can take over the apartment," Niral said.

"Forget that ghetto pad. I'll get you guys real digs, bro."

The next day, Niral did get out. After his morning prayers, he told his father he needed to go to the bank. When his father inquired further, he admitted he would also go to the library and read the Gita; he wanted to escape from the singing that would flood the house for the entire day.

His father told him he understood and blessed him.

But instead of heading to the library or LedaCorp, he took the train to Long Island City.

As he descended the train station stairs, a text message appeared on his phone. It was from Detective Savard. "VISHAL DNA NO MATCH."

Niral cursed into the air. Immediately, he called Detective Savard, who said he'd be testing Amrat's DNA next.

Despite the setback, Niral was undeterred from his mission. He avoided looking at the graffiti building or the girls and went straight to the church building.

He acknowledged Ole and took the elevator to Stan's floor.

When he tried the door, he found it locked. Walking down the hallway, he ran into Lance vacuuming the floor.

"Brother, it's been days. Where you been? I heard you got fired?"

"Long story. I can't get into it now," Niral said, rushing past him.

"You even remember that night? You were crazy recruiting."

"Later..."

"Meet me down at Tony's. You know my spot."

Niral continued down the hallway and turned a couple of times into a labyrinth of hallways until he reached the main office. Father McNally's secretary, Tracy, was typing something. Niral used to hand the rent checks to her.

"Is Father McNally busy?" Niral asked.

"Niral," she said, "I didn't realize you were still working for Stan."

"It's important. Kind of my own venture. You think he would see me?"

"He was on a call, but I'll see."

She called Father McNally, and a few minutes later, Niral was inside his cozy office, lounging on a plush maroon chair.

"I've never been in here," Niral confessed.

"You didn't think a priest could live so well, did you?" Father McNally asked, leaning back on his own chair. "What can I do for you? I was sorry to hear you left Stan's employ."

"I've got something else to talk to you about. Coleman Investments."

The priest's face turned red.

"Yes?"

"Have you heard of it?"

"I'm not sure I'm at liberty to discuss it. Why do you inquire?"

"How about LedaCorp?"

He laughed defensively. "Where are you going with this, Niral?"

"I work for Vishal Patel now. He sent me. Now, do you know it?"

Father McNally didn't answer at first.

"Does he have a message for me?" he finally asked.

"He'd like your answer."

"I thought I already told him. We've discussed it in-depth."

"He wants to make sure."

Father McNally swallowed and seemed to consider his answer.

"If the conditions he proposes are right, if the church will be relocated, I've told him his offer is good."

"For the same price?"

"Does he want more?"

"Are you willing to give more?"

"I would have to speak to him about it," he said. Niral noticed he was now trembling. "I'm afraid I'm just too indisposed at the moment to speak clearly. I didn't expect there would be further terms."

Niral stood. "Thank you, Father. I'll tell Mr. Patel to be in touch with you."

As Niral left the office, Father McNally stood up too, confused and shaking.

58

Niral charged down the hallway and ran into Lance again.

"Back already?"

"Can you open that door for me?" Niral asked, pointing to Lorenzo's Investigations.

"Why?"

"I left something inside. I need to get it."

Lance turned off the vacuum.

"Anything for my right-hand man," he said.

Once inside, Niral checked to see if Stan was there, but the office was empty. Then he went straight to the computer and emailed himself the Quickbooks files, both the company's and Stan's personal account.

Lance lingered in the doorway.

"Just say when," he said.

"You can go to the diner if you want. I'll meet you there."

"Make sure you close up," he responded.

When Lance was gone, Niral unlocked the safe and removed the Macaday file. He found some paperwork and perused it quickly.

Then he opened the envelope containing the surveillance photos.

What he saw shocked him. Photos of Vishal and Mr. Macaday leaving a restaurant were familiar to Niral, but Mr. Macaday's lady friend was there, too.

It was Lauren.

He put the photos in the envelope and resealed it. He placed everything back as he had found it and relocked the safe.

59

Downstairs, Lance was chatting with Ole.

"What you want this time?" Lance asked Niral. "Onion rings?"

"Just come with me," Niral said, "I need your help."

"You better believe this is coming out of your bonus."

As Niral charged toward the graffiti building and the girls, Lance revised his opinion.

"Oh, you meant this kinda help. This is upping your earnings, brother."

Niral asked Lance to stand outside, said he'd be back soon, and told him to make sure no one strange followed him inside.

When he knocked on the door, the asshole opened it, leading out one girl as he prepared to call for more.

Niral passed him and entered the building. As he began climbing the stairs, he heard the asshole's squeaky voice behind him.

"You live here, man?" he asked.

Niral stopped, then turned.

"I'm visiting a friend."

"Gotta make sure. You don't seem the type."

"What type?"

"Kinda like a suit guy. We don't like that in here."

"That's too bad."

Niral turned away abruptly and resumed climbing. Then he felt his shirt being pulled from the back.

"Don't fucking walk away from me," the asshole yelled, grabbing

Niral's right arm. Niral swung around and clocked the asshole with his left fist, but he only got the side of his forehead, so the asshole rebounded, punched Niral in the stomach and pulled him down the stairs. Niral landed hard on the floor and struggled against the asshole who had jumped on top of him and whose hands were now trying to press Niral's face in.

But soon the weight lifted, and the hands disappeared. When Niral looked up, he saw Lance holding the asshole by his shoulders.

"Go ahead, brother," he said, "I got you covered."

Niral didn't look back. He jumped up and rushed up the stairs, passing a couple of skinny artists wearing paint-smeared shirts who reminded him of Jeremy. After pausing to pant for a few seconds, he got to what he believed was Lauren's studio. But he found the door closed.

"You know if this is Lauren's studio?" he asked another skinny artist walking past.

"If Lauren is Cherry Fairy, fuck yeah."

He opened the door and found the room empty. It was how he had left it, except the floor was covered with thin, crisscrossed lines of paint, and the portrait of Amrat was slashed with several, thick black jabs of paint. Across it was scrawled the word: FRAUD.

Niral paced around a bit, searching for clues of where she might have gone. When he couldn't find any, he picked up a paintbrush and wrote over the wall: WHORE.

60

After he had asked a couple of other artists when Lauren might return and got no answers, he went back down the stairs and found Lance outside, chatting with some of the girls. The asshole was nowhere to be found.

"I had a little convo with him, and he took a direct exit back to wherever the fuck he came from," Lance explained. "Don't be messing with the big dogs."

Lance headed toward Tony's, but Niral told him he wanted to check something at Stan's office again before they ate. Lance rolled his eyes but followed Niral.

"You better stop leaving shit in Stan's office, otherwise I'm gonna get fired. I already did too much of Stan's dirty laundry."

When they got up to the room, they found it didn't need unlocking. A semicircle had been carved out of the opaque glass bearing the agency's name, and when Niral tried it, the door was unlocked.

Inside, files were scattered all over the floor, and both PCs had been smashed. Niral noticed the safe door had been ripped open, and the entire Macaday file was missing.

As he scavenged the floor looking for it, and while Lance cursed at the scene, two men wearing trench coats entered the room.

They showed their badges: Detectives Sanchez and Lawrence. Niral and Lance identified themselves. Niral told them he had been Stan's assistant and that his father was a retired police officer.

"I've got bad news for you, Niral," Sanchez said. "We just fished a body out of the East River, less than a mile from here. ID inside the pocket says it's Stan Lorenzo."

61

They made the ID of the body on the rocky shore of the East River underneath the Pepsi-Cola sign.

"Should I call my father and tell him?" Niral asked.

Lance shook his head, dumbfounded.

"I don't know, man. If you can bear it."

Niral put his phone to his ear, but his attention was concentrated on the other side of the river on a single skyscraper.

PART V

Inside the bar across from Vishal's apartment building in Murray Hill, drinks in their hands, Niral and Lance waited to pounce. Finally, they saw Lauren emerge from Vishal's building carrying a black leather bag like the first time Niral saw her. Without giving the bartender a second glance, they left their drinks and followed. Across the steaming streets and FDR Drive, past the police trailers and onto the pier, they all climbed aboard the boat.

Lauren was seated at one end, so they stayed on the other, quietly observing as the boat began accelerating. Niral saw a familiar figure seated across from Lauren, a skinny, tall male, and next to him, a couple of burlier figures.

A few minutes later, the skinny male stood up, strolled across, and sat next to Lauren. She pushed him the bag with her leg. He glanced inside. After placing his hand on her knee and kissing her cheek, he returned to his original seat, holding the bag.

The wind became stronger, and pellets of water hit Niral's face when he noticed one of the burlier figures staring straight at him. He tried to glance away, but from the corner of his eye, he noticed the two figures approach.

"Aren't you the guy—" they started saying, but suddenly Lance was in front of them. Niral scooted past and rushed toward the skinny male, who reached inside his shirt and pulled out a gun. Niral jumped on top of him. He dropped the bag, and wads of strapped bills fell out. They began to struggle.

Lauren screamed.

As the boat continued toward The Dock, they rolled on the floor until the skinny male, now recognizable as Martin, grabbed Niral by the shirt and hoisted him onto the edge of the boat.

With his back pushed against the metal railing, Niral clutched onto a metal ring as he felt the water surging over his neck.

"I'm gonna finish you, you fucking punk," Martin shouted as he smacked Niral's arm with karate chops, trying to force him to let go of the ring. Niral closed his eyes and imagined a watery grave.

"Don't kill him!" he heard behind him. Niral opened his eyes.

Lauren held the gun, and it was pointed directly at Martin. The bag, apparently reconstituted, was in Lauren's other hand. "Let The Manager talk to him."

Martin cursed but pulled Niral in and threw him on the floor. Then he kicked him in the stomach—hard.

Niral coughed and spit blood. Curled sideways on the floor with fuzzy vision, he saw Lance being tag-teamed by the bouncers.

63

The boat docked near the side entrance of the restaurant. Martin and the two bouncers dragged Niral and Lance into the manager's office, their hands tied behind their backs. Lauren wasn't there.

"You come to my restaurant to beat up my staff?" the manager asked, seated behind his desk, his scar prominent and imposing.

"I'm an investigator," Niral explained, coughing and breathing deeply as Martin forced him into a chair.

"You're nothing but a phony," the manager corrected. "And you're poking your nose into the wrong avenues. Things that don't concern you."

"I'm concerned about two dead bodies, sir."

"What two?"

"Vishal's girlfriend and my boss. They found him just yards away in the river."

"I don't know anything about that."

"But you know Vishal. You're getting money from him. Or something."

The manager stood up.

"I'm a businessman. We do business. That's all you need to know. Believe me when I tell you, investigator, that you're in way over your head. Now I'm telling you once and only once more, stay out of my establishment and out of my business. Or you will end up like your boss."

"So you did kill Stan?" Lance asked.

"It's just a statement," the manager replied. "Take it for what it means: a warning. Now get out."

The bouncers pulled them up by their shirts, dragged them outside, threw them to the ground, and kicked them a couple of times. Then, they cut the ropes that bound their hands and shut the door.

64

The guys at the garage across the street stared at them as Niral and Lance stumbled down the wide alley leading to the Citibank building. A couple of them followed steadily, their shadows creeping up the sidewalk behind them. But somehow, as they turned into curving streets, Niral and Lance eluded their pursuers and made their way to Tony's Diner.

The waitress, Martha, got them some napkins and towels, and asked if they wanted her to call the cops.

Niral declined. Lance ordered the special.

"I don't get it," Lance said. "Why's Cherry involved in this whole thing?"

"She's in up to her eyeballs. Involved with every fucking guy in this picture."

"She saved your life, brother. Don't forget that."

"Yeah, I know," he said, shaking his head, remembering what he'd written in Lauren's studio. "I don't understand. It must be Vishal's money. Lauren wouldn't have that kind of cash—unless she's been selling it to every rich dude on Craigslist."

"You think?"

"Doesn't matter, I guess. But why would Vishal be sending a bag of cash to some restaurant owner? If he wanted, he could just wire it or write a check."

"Cash is untraceable. It's under the table."

"But for what? It's got to be this whole Coleman Investments thing.

Vishal is trying to buy the church building. Coleman already owns the restaurant and that art building and Gigglies. Meanwhile, Vishal is sending cash to the restaurant. It's a whole cycle."

He called Martha over.

"Is the owner here today?" he asked.

"He's off tonight. He'll be in tomorrow."

"You know if some Indian guy came in here to speak to him?"

Martha racked her brain. "Come to think of it, yeah. A few times. Talked to Mr. Lombardi in the back."

Niral thanked Martha and turned back to Lance.

"See, he's all over. But why? Vishal makes millions just by sitting behind a desk. His minions do everything for him. He wouldn't be caught dead in Long Island City otherwise, and to come alone? Something's not right. There's got to be some big connection."

"And Stan?"

"I guess he got caught in the middle. You know anything about his personal life? Finances?"

"He's like me: tight with the alimony. He's gotta pay two wives instead of one. No way he was rolling in it. In the old days, he spent his cash at Gigglies, but it's been a while."

"I noticed he hadn't paid the rent from the company account in a few months. Any chance he was paying it out of his personal account?"

"I doubt that. But you know how Father McNally is, always giving people a break. He's a priest, for God's sakes."

"But if Vishal bought the building, Stan might have to pay it all back. And if they demolished the building, Stan might be looking for a new office for new work."

"Where you going with this, brother?" Lance asked as his meal was delivered.

"What if Stan knew Vishal wanted to buy the building? Maybe he saw Vishal inside McNally's office, heard what they were saying, and got concerned. Then when he took the shots of Macaday, Lauren, and Vishal, he made the connection and used the pictures to blackmail Macaday into pressuring Coleman to lay off the building? With evidence of infidelity, Macaday's wife could take half his assets and ruin the financing. And somehow Vishal or someone else working with Coleman found out and got rid of him?"

"You really think Stan would blackmail someone?"

"Would he go against his client?"

"The man wasn't the fondest of wives."

"I feel like it's got to have something to do with those pictures. Otherwise, why would they steal them?"

"Ole said two burly guys went up. Guido types. Kind of like those bouncers at The Dock."

"Possible. All possible. God, this is getting crazy. I'm taking a second to pray."

He did, closing his eyes and reciting the prayers under his breath. He thought of Lauren, and regretting what he had scribbled, asked for forgiveness in his mind as he uttered the Sanksrit phrases. Lance listened respectfully.

"That's beautiful," he said, stuffing his mouth with beef. "Wish I could say that shit at church. Now what we gonna do?"

"Why not wait for the bleeding to stop and ask at the horse's mouth?" Niral suggested.

65

Mr. Macaday's mansion was in a quiet Forest Hills neighborhood, yet not far from the chaos of Queens Boulevard, making it ideal real estate. A Lincoln town car and a Mercedes were parked in the driveway.

Niral and Lance headed up the stairs between two protective stone Lions and onto a marble colonnade. Niral knocked on the door as Lance crouched next to it, ready to pounce.

It was after one a.m., all the lights in the neighborhood were off except the porch lights, and the Macaday household was no exception. Niral made sure to ring the bell several times. Then, he held it down.

The lights flicked on, and Niral heard something slide.

Then a gasp.

The door cracked open. Mrs. Macaday's eye appeared.

"What are you doing here?" she hissed.

"Special delivery," Niral said.

"What?"

"I've got information on your case."

"Does Mr. Lorenzo know you're here? My husband is home, you fool!"

He could hear a man's voice in the background. "Linda?"

Niral gave Lance the cue. He pushed the door forcefully. Mrs. Macaday flew back and began to scream, but Lance clasped his mouth over hers as he grabbed her from behind.

"Gulf war," he said. "That's where I learned it."

Niral entered, shut, and locked the door. As Mrs. Macaday struggled underneath Lance's grip, he massaged her breast with his free hand. She ceased, eyes wide open.

"She thinks the black man's a savage after her flesh," Niral said.

Mr. Macaday stood at the bottom of a spiral staircase, clutching the string of his bathrobe, his face white as alabaster.

"Please, leave us alone," he pleaded. "If you want money, you can take it. I'll even open the safe."

"I just want to talk to you, Mr. Macaday," Niral said. "It's about your wife."

"Talk to me about Linda?"

Niral nodded at Lance. He pulled Mrs. Macaday up the stairs. This time she did struggle, but Lance whispered into her ear, and she stopped. Niral saw tears streaming down her cheeks.

"Don't worry, Mr. Macaday, he won't hurt her," Niral said. "We're not all apes."

Lance winked as he led her up the stairs and disappeared. Niral gestured to Mr. Macaday to lead the way. He was still shaking, but he led Niral into a large dining room and sat down. With a careless shake of his hand, he gestured for Niral to sit across from him.

Niral bowed respectfully and did as requested.

"I believe you know a friend of mine," Niral said. "Vishal Patel."

"Yes, I do invest in Mr. Patel's fund," Mr. Macaday answered, uncomfortably crossing his legs.

"I believe you also know one of Mr. Patel's lady friends."

Mr. Macaday cleared his throat. "So you know about it, then?"

Niral looked at him curiously.

m"No. What should I know?"

146

66

Outside, Niral told Lance he didn't think Macaday was directly involved.

"He seems too out of it. More likely Stan blackmailed Vishal directly."

"If he did."

"What time is it?"

"Two. What are you thinking?"

"I'm thinking about who's open this time of night."

Lance smiled. "Thought you'd never ask, my brother."

They didn't have a tough time getting into Gigglies. Lance asked the madam if Cherry was in. She scowled at Niral.

"She's in the back. I'll see if I can get her."

The large blonde, Candy, came over. Suddenly, two bouncers surrounded Niral and asked if he would come inside for a moment. Niral asked if Lance could accompany him, but they insisted he go alone.

They took him through the back door and to the right, through a long hallway, and then into a single office that was nearly empty except for a desk, a laptop, a calculator, and a clock.

Behind the desk was The Manager. To his left, the madam, to his right, Lauren.

"I made it clear that you shouldn't come around my premises," he said.

"I didn't realize you owned this place too," Niral replied.

"Now you know. And Cherry works for me, so don't try to see her here or anywhere else, or I will follow through on my promise, on you and your entire family. Now go take your nigger friend and get out of here."

Niral stared at Lauren the entire time he spoke, but she looked at the floor, only glancing up once. In sorrow, Niral thought.

67

Lance suggested they hail a cab and head to his place in St. Albans. Niral agreed.

"It might be a good place to lay low if they come looking for us," he said.

As they drove through the residential neighborhood and stopped at Lance's single-story home, Niral expressed surprise.

"You've got a nice house."

"What'd you expect? A housing project, cracks vials on the ground? Man, my momma bought this house in 1973 when there wasn't a black man around."

He let Niral in and immediately they heard a shout from above.

"Daddy, that you?"

"Who you think it is, Santa Claus? That's my daughter, Shoquanda. Believe me, you'll be acquainted soon enough."

He told Niral to wait in the living room while he got something from the basement. When he came back, he held a gun in his hand.

"Old 9 mm, but it should work."

"Licensed?"

"Fuck yeah. Animals come around, they'll be getting a legal bullet in their behinds."

Niral took the gun. It was heavy, but he'd held his father's guns when he was a teenager, so he had some experience. Still, he had never fired one.

Lance made the sofa up with some bedsheets.

"Listen, I gotta go to work in just a couple of hours. Boss has been on my back; I got no choice. Otherwise, he give Eduardo overtime, and I'm not about to lose that. So you're on your own till tomorrow night, but I got an extra key for you. You'll see Shoquanda in the morning. Just make sure she go to school. Otherwise, I got another reason to send her down to her aunt in Carolina."

Niral put the gun under the pillow. Lance threw a gun holster onto the couch, too.

"We've got to plot our course," Niral said.

"You've got to do it, my brother. I got my cell if you need me, but for now, I'm sleeping."

68

Niral woke with a start. He pulled the gun out from underneath his pillow. He saw a black tween in front of him.

"Mista, don't shoot!"

"What the fuck?"

"There's someone at the door."

He heard the knock. Niral told Shoquanda to go into the kitchen. She grinned mischievously, paused, then followed instructions.

"Who is it?" he called out. He heard Shoquanda laughing from the kitchen.

"Be quiet," he told her. "Who is it?" he asked again.

From beyond the door, he heard a soft female voice. When he reiterated his question, and she answered again, he realized it was Lauren.

Swiftly, he approached the door, opened it, and pulled her inside, then checked the vicinity to make sure it was clear.

"What do you want?" Niral asked as he shut the door and locked it.

"To talk," Lauren replied. She wore a tight black dress and black hat. Their lips were close, and he desperately felt like kissing her, but he heard Shoquanda giggling in the background and withdrew.

"Shoquanda, right?" he said, turning to her. "This is Auntie Lauren."

"Your booty call!" she shouted.

"What's it your business?" Niral scolded, but Lauren slapped him on the shoulder to quiet him. She tried to sweet talk Shoquanda, asking her about school. Shoquanda told Lauren she hated school and that she still played with

Barbies.

"But see, Barbie's white. And her best friend's black. So I..."

"Don't you have to go to school?" Niral asked.

Shoquanda got mad and folded her arms.

"Who put you in charge, mista?" she asked, then grabbed her bag and hightailed it out the door before Niral could respond.

"Cute kid," Lauren said. "Yours?"

"Does she look like mine? How'd you know I was here?"

"Candy. She's been here before with Iceman."

"I see. Sit down."

She sat on the sofa. Niral continued to stand, gun still in his shaking hand.

"What's with the outfit?" he asked.

"Trying to fit in."

"I think you'll have to wear blackface for that."

"That's so racist, Niral."

"Just a joke. I'm allowed to joke, right?"

"You're mad."

"Why are you here?"

"I want to warn you about The Manager."

"I'm warned."

"I'm not sure you realize what you'd gotten yourself into. He's a Lucchese."

"Really? Well enlighten me. How'd a Yale girl get involved?"

"I was desperate for money, Niral. I couldn't sell my art. I couldn't go back to my parents. They didn't even know where I'd gone. Vishal came to see me at the club. He saved me from a boyfriend who was using me to buy coke. And that's how everything started."

"The hooking. But you were already stripping."

"You know about that?"

"Mr. Macaday. The investors. Vishal's lackeys. You were blowing them all."

"You make it sound so crude. It was tit-for-tat."

"Business."

"Yes. Some of us need the money."

"Okay. Why don't you tell me about the money Vishal gives The Manager?"

"They'll kill me."

"What do you think I'm going to do?"

"You love me."

"Do I?"

"I hope you do."

"I've got a girl."

"They've all betrayed me. Or used me. I don't have anybody."

"Tell me why Vishal gives money to The Manager."

"He owes The Manager money. That's all I know. All I want to know. Vishal gives me some extra cash for doing it."

"And you work for them both. You're the middle girl."

"All alone in the middle."

"How about my boss? Do you know anything about that?"

Lauren shook her head.

"So you're useless."

"I want to help. I do. That's why I loved Amrat. I want to be better."

"Tell me about Priya. Did she know about the prostitution?"

"Unless she was blind..."

"Was she the madam?"

"What?"

"Did she order you around? Set up appointments?"

"No. She was Vishal's girl, that's all. She would come on individual dates, but she wouldn't be there for the orgies."

"How was she around him?"

"Courteous. Respectful."

"But they weren't in love?"

"She was the dutiful girlfriend," Lauren said. "That's why I have a hard time believing she didn't know. But she wasn't hands on."

"And you never saw her before October?"

"Never. Only after they started dating. Almost like they just made some contract to be together. She did seem kind of cold underneath, like her niceness was just an act. Maybe she was in on it. I don't know."

Niral took a deep breath, then lowered himself to his knees. Lauren began crying.

"I'm sorry, Niral. For all this. I didn't mean for anything to happen, I swear. I was in over my head too."

Slowly, Niral put his gun on the floor. Then, he reached his arms out to her.

She went down to her knees too and crawled over to him. She awkwardly touched his face, then clasped onto him.

They hugged for a long time.

She began to pull away, but his lips met hers.

Slowly, they shed each other's clothes. He kissed her breasts softly, then kissed her belly button with sweet pecks. Suddenly, their motions became more fierce and animalistic, until they stopped making love and began fucking, changing positions frequently, Niral hurling Lauren's body around.

They finished doggy-style.

They came and crumbled to the floor in despair. Lauren held Niral's arm around her tightly and cried. Behind her and still inside her, he buried his face in her shoulder.

"What am I going to do with you?" he asked.

"Nothing," she responded, wiping away a tear. "But I want to help you."

He kissed her strongly on her salty cheek once, then disengaged from her body and lay flat on his back, staring up at the ceiling, while she stayed sideways, as if in a cocoon.

Once they had dressed, Niral, while pacing around, asked her, "When are you showing in Chelsea?"

"I'm not. I quit," she said, putting on her hat as she sat on the floor. "I'm just a slut now. Nothing else."

"But the art's there for display?"

"I destroyed the art in my studio. I'm going to do the same thing there."

"Don't. Show it. Make sure Vishal and Mr. Macaday are there. Can you do that?"

"If it helps you, Niral," she said, standing up. "But be careful. The Manager will know if you talk to Vishal."

"But if Vishal is scared of The Manager, maybe he won't tell."

"Will you do something for me, Niral?" she asked, approaching.

"What?"

"Ask Amrat to meet me. He won't return my phone calls."

"He told me you were avoiding him."

"At first," she said, grabbing Niral's arms. "But now I need him in my

157

life. And he thinks I betrayed him. Everyone thinks that."

Niral swallowed and thought.

"Okay, I'll do it," Niral said, tipping her hat back. "But only if you help me."

Niral noticed he had several missed calls from his father, so he called back.

"Are you okay, Niral?" his father asked.

"Yeah. I'm staying with a friend. I've got a lead on Stan's death."

"Be careful, Niral. I never told you to play policeman. Just come back and pray for Bhen's soul with us."

"I've got a good lead, Deddy. I know you're devastated by Stan's death. I'm going to make you proud."

"Niral—"

Niral hung up.

Niral called Detective Savard.

"Not Amrat's DNA either," Savard informed him.

"I know," Niral replied.

"You think you know who did it?"

"I've got a lead," Niral said. "I'll be in touch."

71

Niral took the bus to Flushing. Behind the Korean church, he trekked down an alley past a karaoke bar and up steep stairs to a spa. He pressed the button.

A woman's voice said something in Korean. He said, "Is Wan here?"

After a pause, he was buzzed in. An older woman, a madam he supposed, was standing behind a counter. She looked at him strangely. Then she asked him for the password again in English.

"Is Wan here?" he repeated.

"That is not password."

"Wan. Korean guy. Used to have a wave," Niral said, flipping his hand past his head. "Now he's bald, I think."

"No Wan here. You been here before?"

Niral didn't answer.

"Fine," the madam said. "You friend of Wan, you pay house fee now. You want massage, right?""

A young Korean woman come out of a room, holding a towel, and smiled at him coyly. Then another door opened, and a young Korean man emerged.

"Gandhi, you making trouble?"

"Where's Wan, Ricky?"

Ricky studied him. "Niral?"

Niral pointed his gun at him.

Ricky checked his pants quickly for his own weapon, then held his

161

hands up.

"Whoa, hold it, man!"

Then, through the same door, another young man emerged.

"Niral. My main man," Wan said.

72

Inside a dusty room, a few Korean gangsters sat around a poker table. To the side, Wan, Ricky, and Niral hunched around an overturned oil can. Ricky smoked a cigarette.

"When I said I'd get you a gig, I didn't mean coming here with a gun, man."

"I need your help. You do business with the Italians?"

"We do business with whoever helps us and doesn't step on our toes."

"How about a guy named The Manager?"

"He have a first name?"

"That's all I have."

"Sounds familiar," Ricky said. "He's pretty high up with the Lucchese, kinda shadowy, legit on the surface."

"I need to be able to get to him if I can. A real name, a home address, if possible. Somewhere he's vulnerable."

"You gonna do a hit?"

"Not exactly. I just need the info."

Wan and Ricky looked at each other.

"We can ask higher ups and get what you want," Wan said. "But what are you offering in return?"

"Remember in junior high, when I distracted those black kids from mugging you? After you joined the Dragons, you said if anyone ever messed with me, to tell you and you'd take care of it? Well, someone's messing with me. I need to take care of it. But it's just a name and address I want."

"Junior high was a long time ago, bro."

"Just a name and address."

Ricky snickered. "Fucking herb."

But Wan stuck his fist out at Niral.

"Fine, but you owe me. My nigga," he said.

73

Outside the Chelsea art gallery, with Lance behind the wheel of Niral's car, Niral waited in the back seat for Mr. Macaday to emerge with Lauren.

When she did, she winked at Niral.

He got out of the car and snuck inside the gallery. He approached Vishal while he was viewing one of Lauren's surrealist paintings entitled "Dharma" featuring a group of vague, masked figures holding hands around a fire.

"She's got talent," Niral said.

Vishal, holding a glass of champagne, seemed pleased to see him.

"A little too grotesque for me. I can see how someone as sophisticated as you might like it," he said.

"I don't think I've ever received a compliment from you, Vishal," Niral responded.

Vishal contemplated him for a long while.

"Must be because you're part of the family now."

"Was Priya part of the family?"

"Of course."

"Your dad knew about her. Your mom had Sunday dinners with her. You were all happy."

Vishal's smile was frozen.

"I'm not catching your drift," he said.

"We both know she was a hired girlfriend or something. Just like you hired Lauren. Just like you hire everybody. Is that why you killed Stan? Because you couldn't buy him?"

Before Vishal could react, Niral stuck a gun into his back.

"Shut up and walk out the door. Tell your driver you're going home with me, and act natural or I'll fucking blow a hole through you."

74

When they were in Middle Village, Niral forced Vishal into a cemetery. Lance followed for backup.

Niral pushed him back with the gun. Vishal tripped over a tombstone and almost landed into a large hole, but he scampered away from it as Niral approached.

"That's for Stan," Niral said, kicking him back on his ass as he tried to stand. "Maybe we should bury you with him."

"You've got it all wrong, Niral," Vishal said. "You really are a Kshatriya."

"I looked at Stan's personal Quickbooks account, asshole. I emailed it to myself before your thugs destroyed his computer. He had written in a payment from you for one hundred thousand. He liked to anticipate and calculate incoming funds before they arrived. That was his blackmail fee for the picture of Macaday and Lauren. But it never came. He thought it was for adultery. But really it was for prostitution. And your whole fucking project."

Vishal stood on his knees.

"You've got it all wrong, Niral."

"Explain it, then," Niral said, pointing the gun at Vishal's head.

"That's all right. I'm not saying it isn't. But I didn't kill anybody. It was all The Manager. He's blackmailing me too. That's why I send the cash with Lauren."

"Bullshit," Niral said.

"You don't know my side, man. I don't need the fucking money. I got money, the legit way. But The Manager's been leaning on me. He's a fucking Lucchese. He forced me to invest in this Long Island City thing and to buy up the property. I don't know anything about real estate. Once the mob gets their claws in you, you can't get out. They run the construction unions, the OTBs, they've got influence on the community board."

"What about Priya?"

"The Manager heard about the argument with Amrat, in a public place, in his place with Priya. If anybody found out about the prostitution thing, the dominoes would roll on the whole enterprise. So, he got rid of Priya to teach me a lesson. He even sent a message, a bouquet of roses, the next morning. Like a stab in the eye."

"What did the argument with Priya have to do with prostitution?"

"She was running the hooker front. That's what turned her on. She set everything up from behind the scenes. If Priya told Amrat, everything would be done."

"Why didn't The Manager kill Amrat too?"

"I don't know, Niral. I guess he just wanted to hurt me bad, to send me a message. I've been on the hook for a long time. And Priya had to die for it. So did your boss."

"What did The Manager do for you that he got you hooked?"

Vishal lowered his head. "He helped me out with money."

"For LedaCorp? So you didn't win big on the housing collapse?"

"I did. But first, I had to build up capital to get Carty's investors to come over to me. That allowed me to pay them returns before I'd actually earned anything."

"A Ponzi scheme?"

"I wasn't stealing from anybody. It was just a loan. I paid The Manager

168

back when I won big. But he didn't just want the principal—he wanted interest. So, he forced me into this whole Coleman thing. Interest."

"But you're gonna make it big if the project goes through."

"He'll get most of it. I'm a hedge fund guy, Niral. I know about virtual buying and selling. I'm not interested in the specifics of real estate."

Niral shook his head.

"Why should I believe you?" he asked.

"You don't have to," Vishal insisted. "But it's the truth."

"Get up," Niral ordered. "You're gonna come with me and tell Detective Savard. He'll get the truth out of you."

Vishal raised his arms and got up slowly.

"He'll put me in witness protection, right?"

"If what you say is true."

"I don't want my life to change forever without seeing Meetal perform at Shri Holi, Niral. It's tonight."

Niral paused.

"I forgot about that," Niral admitted, closing his eyes.

"You want to see her, too, right? You think she'll forgive you if we don't go?"

Niral considered what Vishal said, then glanced at Lance.

"He's your hostage," Lance said, shrugging his shoulders. "I'll drive you back, then cab it back to the job. Father McNally's only so forgiving."

75

Shri Holi took place in an elementary school auditorium in Flushing where many Brotherhood meetings and classes were held. Unlike the typical Holi celebration where people threw colors at one another, the Brotherhood celebrated Holi by dramatizing the story of Prahlad and his father, Hiranyakashipu, usually through plays and dance performances put on by young children and teens.

The story that had inspired Holi was an ancient myth about a young boy who had defied his father by believing strongly in the Hindu god, Vishnu. Prahlad's father, Hiranyakashipu, was a king who wanted to be worshipped as a god by all people. Hiranyakashipu tried to murder his son several times. Prahlad was stampeded by elephants, poisoned, thrown off a cliff, and bitten by snakes, but every time, Prahlad's devotion saved him. Finally, his father had his sister, Holika, sit in a bonfire with Prahlad in her lap. Holika had received a boon that protected her from fires, but the flame consumed her anyway, and Prahlad was saved. Hiranyakashipu had received a boon from Brahma exempting him from being killed inside or outside, at morning or night, on land, sea or air, by thrown weapon or held weapon, or by human or animal, but he was eventually killed by Vishnu. Vishnu, incarnated as half-man, half-lion, emerged from a pillar and butchered him in the middle of his home's doorway at twilight, raising him up on his knee and slaughtering him with his claws.

This drama was being enacted by Brotherhood youth as Vishal and Niral entered the auditorium, Niral holding his gun under his jacket and shoving it into Vishal's back. They saw the Brotherhood elders in front, the women and men segregated by sections. They did not see Amrat, and Niral realized he must be meeting Lauren, something he had set up before he confronted Vishal. Niral didn't see Meetal, so he assumed she must have been in the back of the stage, preparing.

They sat on the male side of the auditorium, Vishal in front of him. Kauntiaunti glanced back and nodded at her son. Niral made sure Vishal didn't whisper anything to her, poking his gun into Vishal's side to make sure. On the stage, and even on the surrounding walls, he noticed a plethora of pictures of Bhen, huge portraits garlanded and covered in red kum kum powder.

As the play unfolded, Vishal chuckled at a few miscues, while Niral tried to focus on the task at hand. But when Meetal came on, Niral lost his concentration.

She was beautiful in a red and gold sari, her belly button peeking slightly below her choli, her odhni strategically placed to the side of her face, three fingers ticked up while her thumb index fingers formed a circle like she was signaling okay. Her palms were glittered with gold too, her face ornamented with a touch of blush and perhaps rouge. Her head and body were tilted slightly to the left. A smile emanated from her lips.

It seemed her routine was a hybrid of Bharat Natyam and a Western dance, but the song was a religious one about Holika's upending and Prahlad's triumph, the victory of devotion to dharma over ego and power. As it progressed, Meetal seemed to alternatively be pulled into vice and then turned off by it, making coordinated movements and showing facial expressions that demonstrated a turbulent modern story which seemed to go beyond the typical myth. She appeared to mime an addiction to drinking, an attachment to a man, an obligation to a group that perhaps was not worthy of her devotion. The dance was as much drama as movement, and Niral couldn't help tear up at its power, especially during the final act as Meetal curved down and plastered herself to the floor, her hands and palms out, her legs spread-eagle, her head down like she didn't know which way to go.

Niral stood and clapped while the others waved their hands in the typical Indian way. Her brother didn't stir.

As Niral sat down again and wiped away his tears, Vishal turned to him. "She's good, eh?"

"Shut up," Niral responded, but he realized he couldn't wait to see her after the ceremony.

When all the performances were done, a group of women gathered and led a final prayer. Niral recited it to himself. Then, Narendrakaka climbed onto the stage. He began to read from a piece of paper.

"Thank you for coming," he said in Gujarati. "I would like to first lead another prayer, for Bhen."

The next prayer commenced, and Niral recited it to himself again.

"Bhen has meant so much to us; I cannot say in words how I feel," Narendrakaka continued once the prayer was finished. Then, he began weeping, and he covered his face. Niral's father came up to the stage to console him and patted him on the back.

Niral looked over at Vishal. He appeared emotionless.

Finally, Narendrakaka wiped his tears with a handkerchief and continued. "We will keep up her work, for equality and brotherhood, for an end to division and a return to dharma. I will be retiring from my role, but my brothers in the front row here will do a good job uniting the Brotherhood from across the country and the world for one purpose: to spread Bhen's message. And Bhai, from India, will be a great leader."

There was a great pause, and Niral could hear people weeping.

"Let us remember the great purpose of the Brotherhood. No matter our role in life or how we were born, we are equal, and we must devote our lives to reaching the perfection of consciousness. We all know the tragedy that affected us recently, the passing of our beloved Priya, but we must not let it distract us from our life's purpose, of doing the right thing, of following the right way. Let us—"

But Narendrakaka suddenly stopped. A stir in the back of the auditorium caused everyone to turn around to observe the source of the commotion.

76

In the back of the auditorium, Dilipuncle stumbled around. He was drunk, shirtless, and clad in a dirty white dhoti.

"You killed my Priya," he shouted, pointing at Narendrakaka. "I killed my Priya."

Everyone stood up as he tumbled down the aisle and passed Niral. Unfurling his dhoti and throwing it on the stairs, he climbed on stage naked and, clutching his janoi, lunged at Narendrakaka like he was going to strangle him with it, shouting "Bhen killed my Priya! Bhen killed my Priya!"

Niral's father rushed up and pushed him. Dilipuncle fell back onto the stage.

When he tried to rise again, he began to vomit.

Then he gasped and passed out.

PART VI

Sureshuncle and Premuncle were doctors, so they were able to revive Dilipuncle. He sat up and drank some water. Then, slowly, he told his tale while the others, including Niral, gathered around and listened intently. Niral had lost track of Vishal, but at the moment, he didn't care.

Dilipuncle said it all began when his wife died. Kirtiaunti had been a solid devotee of the Brotherhood, and when she suddenly died of cancer, everyone was devastated. Amrat, who had abandoned the family for a secular academic year at Harvard, seemed to change overnight at the death, becoming dedicated to his own version of the Brotherhood, but Dilipuncle said that Narendrakaka was concerned about him and Priya. Neither had been as devoted to the Brotherhood or to Bhen as their mother, and he was worried not only of their financial well-being but of their spiritual well-being, too.

At the time, Dilipuncle and Kirtiaunti had been thinking of buying a house in Floral Park, but with Kirtiaunti's income gone and Amrat unable to immediately make a difference, Dilipuncle and his family seemed destined to live in the railroad flat in Sunnyside, barely making the rent. It certainly was not an ideal situation for Priya to grow up in.

Narendrakaka came to believe it was his dharma to help the family of such a powerful devotee, so he offered to help Dilipuncle with the mortgage. But Dilipuncle, seeing a good play for himself, demanded that Narendrakaka buy the house for him outright, as that would secure Priya's future and his own devotion to the Brotherhood.

Narendrakaka took the money from the Brotherhood Fund, which at the time was never audited. He believed he had done a holy deed and that eventually other donations would cover up the nearly million-dollar hole.

But when Bhen became ill around Diwali and Bhai wished to unify the Brotherhood financial structure, he had the Fund audited and discovered the fraud. He confronted Narendrakaka, who explained the theft had been executed for good reason. But Bhai would not listen and demanded Narendrakaka pay the money back within two weeks.

Niral knew this was Bhai's effort to discredit Narendrakaka and force him out, even before Bhen's death.

"Vishal saved me," Narendrakaka said softly, sadly. "I could not escape my crime forever, but my son tried."

"How did he save you?" Niral asked.

"He came up with the money and paid the Fund back."

"When was that?"

"Last October," Narendrakaka said. "But he could only delay my karma."

"Vishal could not pay right away," Dilipuncle added. "He did not have the money, he said. He would try to get it together. I became nervous. Not only could Narendrabhai get into trouble, but I could go to jail too. But then, only a few days later, Vishal informed us he had gotten the money."

"The sacrifices a son makes for his father," Narendrakaka said.

"I don't understand," Niral said. "What does this have to do with Priya's death?"

Dilipuncle was quiet at first. Then he explained.

"When Amrat discovered Priya's engagement with Vishal, she became scared that he would eventually find out about the mortgage money. You see, Amrat had been paying the mortgage to us since we had bought the house.

177

We never told him Narendrabhai had paid it off and Priya and I kept it in a separate account for our own uses. When he found out what we had done all those years, about the money we had stolen from him, he was honest enough to tell everyone, and we could lose everything overnight.

"She called me from a pay phone in her dormitory. I came up the back way, like I sometimes did to give her presents. I thought I could calm her down, but she told me horrible things, about how she had set up prostitution of other women to make money. She did not make sense. She said she had prostituted herself too, that she did not want to live anymore. I told her to go to sleep, that Amrat would never find out. She said she would tell him herself, that she was sick of our lying life. I became angry, pleaded with her that she would ruin everything. She said she'd rather kill herself than continue. She went to the window, like she was going to jump. I pulled her back by her odhni. She bounced back to me, but in the struggle, I must have pushed her. I tried to pull her back by the odhni, but she must have..."

The aunties were weeping. So was Niral's mother.

"Why was the door locked?" Niral asked calmly.

"Priya had given me a copy of the key. I locked it after I cleaned off anything I could inside."

Niral watched Meetal. She was sitting on the stage, weeping too. Her eyes were as red as her cheeks, and when she matched Niral's gaze, she leapt up and ran behind the stage.

78

Alkeshuncle asked Niral's father about next steps. Meanwhile, Niral followed Meetal behind the stage. As she charged past the play props, he grabbed her odhni and stopped her.

He reeled her in and felt her warm arms around him. He kissed her intensely. She tried to push him away, then suddenly grabbed his shirt and held on for dear life. Then, she pushed him away again and fell onto a chair, crying.

"It's all been a lie, a lie. I can't believe this."

"You don't know the half of it, Meetal."

"How can it get any worse? My father is ruined. Dilipuncle, too, and on Bhen's special day."

"Do you know where your brother went?"

Meetal looked up angrily.

"My brother? Why do you want to know?"

"He was here, then he left."

"We know everything; why do you want him?"

"I want to talk to him about business."

"Now? Don't lie to me, Niral. There have been enough lies."

"Fine. I need to talk to him about what Dilipuncle said. I'm not sure he heard it."

"He'll hear it. Why don't you be a good man and be with me?"

"I would," Niral said, hesitating. "But there are still some loose ends I need to tie up."

"You're not even on this case. You're supposed to be doing prayers and working with my brother, not investigating a murder that's already been solved."

"In case you hadn't heard, my boss was murdered too, a couple of days ago."

Meetal stood up. "That's not my problem, Niral. When a family is falling apart, you stay with them and help them heal. You don't make more trouble."

"Fine. Then where's Vishal, helping us heal?"

"He saved my father. Or at least he tried to."

"Yes. He's always throwing money at everything."

She slapped him once, hard. He held his cheek, not knowing how he should react. She turned and began to walk away, so he marched in the other direction.

"I'm supposed to fly out tomorrow, Niral!" Meetal shouted. But he didn't wait.

79

Niral drove to Forest Hills and double-parked in front of Mr. Macaday's house. He didn't want to frighten Mrs. Macaday, but it turned out she wasn't there.

Mr. Macaday stood in his driveway, hands in pockets, contemplating his Lincoln town car. He was dressed in a tuxedo, different from the suit he had worn at the gallery.

He noticed Niral approach in the bare light of dusk. He seemed calm.

"She says she is giving up her craft, moving back with her parents in Maine."

"Lauren?"

"I told her she has talent. Plenty of people came to the show. But no one bought anything." He shook his head. "I offered to buy every painting, but she refused, said it wouldn't be legitimate. After all this, she has a sense of honor. I realize now what I did was wrong. She's young; she doesn't even know where she's going in this life. And Linda is a decent woman. Maybe we will work it out after all."

"Does Vishal know she's quitting?"

"I have no idea."

"Did he say where he planned to go after the gallery?"

"He did mention his house in Sands Point."

"Do you know the address?"

"Yes. But it's difficult to find. There are no street signs up there."

Niral held out his hand. "Try me," he said.

Niral left Mr. Macaday next to his town car, put the address into his GPS system, and headed toward the Long Island Expressway. When he reached Port Washington, it was completely dark. He asked someone at the Long Island Railroad station about the location of Vishal's house and received the same warning: "There's no parking up there, and if you pull over on the side, the cops'll bag you fast."

Niral took it under advisement but ventured up Middle Neck Road anyway, through the woods and past the majestic silhouettes of Gothic mansions. He had no idea where Vishal would be, but he decided to play his hunch and hoped it would lead to the promised land.

The GPS system kept telling him to turn around as the road curved ahead, but he went straight anyway, because only one road existed for million-dollar homes. He persevered until he didn't see the silhouettes of homes anymore, just woods and the occasion lane, the GPS now telling him his goal lay ahead.

Suddenly, the road straightened, and when he finally reached the end of it, the GPS system confirmed he was at the right location.

80

He pulled up the windy dirt driveway, up to Vishal's limousine. He killed his lights, then his engine. Besides the chirping of crickets, it was eerily quiet. The mansion loomed above him, up a slight hill.

He got out, opened his trunk, and pulled out a flashlight. Niral knew he should use the flashlight only if necessary. He began to approach the house but then stopped and turned to his left, beyond the shallow woods, to what seemed to be the beach. He saw two figures lingering on the shoreline, each separated by considerable distance.

He put the flashlight back in his trunk and crawled through the woods, careful not to crunch the twigs too loudly and trying to avoid the brush, sharp oak branches and thorns. When he reached the edge of the woods, he realized his caution was groundless because the beach was wide, and anyone could see him coming. He let go of precautions and marched toward the figure at the far end, near the water, making sure his gun was in its proper place: strapped to the holster attached to his waistband. When he turned to check, he no longer saw the other figure.

Vishal was calmly waiting for him, his hands twisted behind his body. He seemed to be contemplating as he watched the calm water.

"My sister called me," he shouted as Niral approached. "She told me Dilipuncle confessed everything. It's not right. It could undermine everything the Brotherhood has strived for."

"You already knew," Niral asserted.

"I thought it was The Manager, Niral. Now, I realize that bouquet was just consolation. I had no clue until now why Priya died. I realize I should have stayed with her that night. I should have told her I knew about the Fund. Amrat would have never figured it out anyway, and what did it matter? I could have provided for all of them."

"Didn't you tell her about financing the Fund when you met her?" Niral asked.

"No," Vishal shrugged. "Why would I do that?"

"Why did you wait to give your father the money in October? First you had it, then you didn't."

"Because I had to borrow it from The Manager."

"In October, you'd already made your fortune on the housing market and from your hedge fund. You'd bought this house, that apartment, all kinds of things that cost millions. Yet you didn't have a measly million dollars to donate to a religious fund?"

"The Manager keeps extorting me, man. I need to keep borrowing to keep up."

"Priya stopped talking to her roommate in October. She got gloomy; she hid your relationship from everybody. She told her father she prostituted herself, yet Lauren said she never participated directly. So that leaves one possibility. You blackmailed her. You told her if she didn't become your girlfriend, you'd ruin her father and her, by allowing your dad to default on Bhai's deadline."

Vishal shook his head.

"That's crazy. Why would I? I could get plenty of women with my money."

"Not every woman is Amrat's sister. You wanted to get back at him for civilizing your hooker, taking her away from you."

"How sick do you think I am?"

"I don't pretend to understand your mind, Vishal. I just know you like to control people with money."

Vishal shifted his hands to his front, locked them in a fist, and made his way toward the water. Niral followed.

"You just don't get it, Niral," he said. "I don't give a shit about Lauren or Amrat. It was the principle."

"What principle? Control?"

Vishal turned viciously toward Niral. "Principle of equality, you fucking asshole. You know, what everyone's been preaching."

"You taught her a lesson in equality by blackmailing her?"

"There is no equality, Niral, and there never will be. Whether it's caste or money or power or class, something will always separate us. There will always be haves and have-nots. Read Masoch: if you have to be the hammer or the anvil, you might as well be the hammer. Priya believed that—until I showed her the tables could be turned."

Vishal tread into the water. Niral became anxious but followed him anyway.

"One summer," Vishal explained, "the one after sophomore year, I came back from Yale to work in the deli. I had to get scholarships, and my dad even had to mortgage the place to get money for tuition. I had to work in that store all summer to save up. I never dreamed I'd get this.

"Meetal was still in high school then, and Priya would come over sometimes to hang out with her at our apartment. One day, I came up after a long shift. Priya was there alone, lounging on the sofa, watching TV. Apparently Meetal had gone out to talk to one of her friends.

"I changed into a nice shirt and pants and returned to the living room.

She joked that I wasn't wearing my Sudra clothes anymore.

"I sat with her and we talked about our dreams of working at i-banks. She kept bragging that her dad kept buying her Gucci bags and Razr cellphones. I said good for her. She told me she wanted to earn it one day, to buy it all herself.

"I have to say, that was a turn-on—an ambitious girl—and she was pretty cute. She was underage, but I was a teenager, too, and the difference was so small, I guess I didn't think about it. So, I leaned in and kissed her. She pushed me back and spit in my face."

The water was now above Niral's knees. "Because you were a creepy older guy?"

Vishal put one arm on Niral's shoulder. "Because I was a dirty Vaishya, she said. She was better than me; she would always be better than me. After all that crap about equality, she told me that, Niral. And she meant it, too. But the world was changing. It had changed. And I was older. I'd get the wealth first."

"She was a kid, Vishal. Kids say stupid things. They have dumb prejudices."

"I was a kid, too. That doesn't make it right. I taught that bitch dharma. And I'm going to teach you, Niral, to reach your karma. You still believe you're superior, don't you?"

"I never did…" Niral started, but then a sharp pain hit Niral's stomach. He lurched over to see a knife in his belly. Seconds later, he was under water.

He struggled by kicking, but this only landed him supine on the ocean floor, Vishal's weight on him. He gritted his teeth to keep from swallowing, but he felt Vishal wrenching his mouth open. Niral reached for his gun, but before he could remove the weapon, he impulsively pushed Vishal as his

186

mouth was forced open and a flood rushed in.

He felt like he was drowning: he saw a flash of white light and a spiraling vortex. By reflex, he must have kneed Vishal because Vishal let go of him and jumped up. Just as quick, Niral reached the gun holster, unclipped it, and pointed up. He felt Vishal land on him again as he closed his eyes and pulled the trigger.

He heard a brief yelp, like a puppy's cry. Instinctively, he pushed up, moving Vishal's body away. He balanced himself on the ocean floor as he came to the surface, spitting out the salt water, karate chopping and coughing desperately until he was free. Then, he waded toward shore.

As he spat out the remaining water, Niral tried to regain his sense of place. The cold wind hit him in the face as he glanced back and saw Vishal sitting in the water, holding his crotch. Then Niral couldn't see him anymore, just the vast ocean and the black abyss of the sky beyond it.

Niral crawled out of the water and began to stumble back to the woods, holding onto the gun. Suddenly, he saw a figure running toward him in the distance. Niral pointed his gun and fired, the backward thrust of the shot almost causing him to drop the weapon.

The figure ducked, then crouched and fired back. Niral raced toward the woods, and when he turned, he saw the figure still dashing toward him.

Coughing and breathing laboriously, the knife still sticking out of his stomach, he got into his car and turned on the engine. He fired one last shot out of the window to force the figure, now in the woods, to duck again as Niral pulled out of the driveway.

The limo followed him all the way onto the Long Island Expressway before Niral was able to lose him by swerving in and out of lanes and jamming it up behind some large trucks. By the time Niral pulled off onto Utopia Parkway, he was gasping for air and had to double park to regain his energy. His stomach was stinging, and he was losing blood, but if he pulled out the knife, he knew he would probably bleed more. Hot sweat dripped from his brow, he felt cold shivers, and he spat large gobs of blood onto the dashboard.

He drove down Utopia, made it to Northern Boulevard and to Flushing. He parked next to a fire hydrant and climbed up to the spa as he saw stars.

He pressed the button and yelled the password in Korean, which Wan had given him. He was buzzed into the building. As he entered, he heard a woman scream as he collapsed on the floor and blacked out.

When he awoke, Niral found himself tied to a chair. Ricky waved Niral's gun in his face, while Wan leaned over to make sure he was awake.

"What happened?" Niral asked drowsily.

"Be glad Ricky here's been pulling knives out of niggas for a while," Wan responded. "He saved your ass."

Niral examined his torso and saw his stomach was bandaged and taped around.

"Thanks," he said, nodding vaguely at Ricky, who repaid him by pushing the gun against Niral's forehead, shoving it back and blowing his breath like he had fired.

"Is there any special reason you called, in your, uh, time of need?" Wan asked, leaning back. "Or did you expect us to be surgeons?"

"He wanted to prove he really is gangsta, right, Niral?" Ricky joked as he twirled the pistol around his finger.

Niral coughed as he took in the empty room, seeing the playing cards scattered around the other table.

"I want what I requested before," he said. "The address."

"Looks like I already paid you back with this assist," Wan replied.

"I would appreciate another favor," Niral insisted, feeling the sting in his stomach.

"Does it have anything to do with this? Because we don't want any trouble with the Italians."

"Don't worry, I won't tell them I got the info from you."

Wan checked with Ricky, and he seemed to give him the go-ahead.

"All right, Niral," Wan said, "we checked around and got a name: Roberto Tragliani. An address in Maspeth. I'll give it to you. Just promise you won't do anything stupid."

"I promise."

"All right. And remember, Niral, now you owe me one."

83

Wearing Ricky's t-shirt, Niral reached a small suburban house in Maspeth around four p.m. He could still see and smell the blood inside his car. He parked in front, got out, and made sure his gun was back in its rightful place.

But it didn't matter because inside he was searched by two goons and relieved of his weapon. He waited in the tiny but comfy and fairly typical suburban living room, seated on a recliner.

Within minutes, The Manager appeared, wearing a tuxedo. He spoke immediately.

"Give me a reason why my guys shouldn't blow you away on the spot and drop your ass in the East River. I told you to stay away from my business, and now you come to my home, unannounced? My daughter just got married last night. She's coming over for dinner in a couple of hours before she goes on her honeymoon. Maybe I should put you on the menu."

"I'm sorry. But I'm here to deal, not to make trouble."

"What kind of hand can you possibly have?"

"I just killed your main ally."

The Manager sat across from Niral.

"Lauren?"

"Vishal Patel."

He pondered Niral for a few seconds.

"You killed Vishal?"

"He's in the Long Island Sound. He tried to kill me, so I fought back."

"I see," The Manager muttered, nodding. "Vishal was a good friend. There was a lot of give and take between me and him. He'll be missed, but it's not catastrophic."

"He's the top investor in Coleman. Without his fund, you've got a huge hole. And what if Mr. Macaday and his other investors pull out?"

"I've got a lot of investors, a lot of friends. And I don't like how much you know."

"My knowledge will stay with me. And you can keep all your money, too, if you take my deal."

"How's that?"

"With Vishal dead, and without a wife, his assets would go to his father, who will probably give it to his sister. And I'm going to marry her. So I could persuade her to let me lead the fund as a figurehead. I know a little, and I can appoint someone under me who can really run things. Bottom line, investors don't run away, and everything keeps going smoothly."

"In return for?"

"Staying alive. My family and me, we aren't harmed. And no more blackmail, no more payments to you, nothing but the investment and what stands. We never meet again."

"I don't know what blackmail you're referring to. And I don't care. You're not going to get any more info about past transactions. But your deal does sound good, as long as it works out the way you say it will. Is there any evidence linking you to Vishal's death?"

"It was self-defense. He stabbed me in the stomach first."

"Self-defense claims can go either way, especially in this state. Were there any witnesses?"

"His chauffeur. But I'm not sure he actually saw it."

"He'll probably disappear and end up in some Latino gang. Did you own the gun you shot him with?"

"No, but your guys took it. You can make it disappear. And you can go to the Long Island Sound and make Vishal's body disappear for good, too."

"I can hold both as collateral in case things don't go as planned. Your deal sounds reasonable. Now get lost before my daughter shows up. You smell like shit."

As Niral stood up, relieved The Manager had agreed to his plan, The Manager's cell phone rang.

"Are you kidding?" he shouted into it. He rose and glared at Niral.

"What happened?" Niral asked.

"Gigglies is on fire. Did you—"

"I have no idea, man," Niral said, holding up his hands. "I swear."

As Niral reached Gigglies, he saw a huge black cloud rising, along with firefighters and scores of the usual scavengers hovered around, from insurance adjustors to boarders. Then, he noticed two other black clouds in the distance, competing with each other.

He drove closer and realized one was the graffiti building. He pulled up to the cordoned area and jumped out. The asshole was being interviewed by Detective Sanchez as firefighters continued to run in and out of the building.

"I saw the smoke, so I went upstairs. It was in that girl Lauren's studio. She was lying on the ground, her eyes were open, man, and her throat had fucking been slashed. And some painting was on fire, and then in like a second, the whole room went up. So, I closed the door and ran out. Someone came over with a water bucket, but I told him it was too late. We had to abandon ship."

Detective Sanchez made eye contact with Niral as Niral jumped back in his car. The detective ran toward him, commanding him to wait, but Niral backed up and sped away.

Niral pulled over on Queens Boulevard in Woodside and took a deep breath. He called his father.

"Where have you been, Niral? We have been worried."

"I'll tell you later. Everything's going to hell."

"What do you mean?"

"Nothing. Did you take Dilipuncle to Savard?"

"No. Dilipuncle fainted again, so we brought him home and put him to bed. Premuncle said we should consult Bhai before we call the police."

"Why?"

"That is the way he wanted it. I told him it was not proper, but one day will not make a difference. Where are you?"

Niral tried to think, but his head was spinning, and he needed a drink of water.

"Who's with him?"

"Sureshuncle was staying with him, but he just called me and said Amrat came back and told him he would look after his father."

"He told Amrat about what happened?" Niral asked, eyeing a deli.

"I think so."

"Okay, Deddy, I'll call you later."

"Be careful, Niral."

"I love you, Deddy," he said and hung up.

By the time Niral parked in front of Dilipuncle's home, it was nearing dusk. He tried the front door and found it unlocked.

The living room was dark and the light switch didn't work, so Niral returned to his car and got the flashlight from his trunk.

Slowly, he proceeded into the house. Flinging around the beam of light, he didn't see anyone in the living room. He checked the kitchen, then the two bedrooms on the ground floor, including Dilipuncle's room, where he found nothing but a made bed and the pictures of Shiva and Laxmi staring back at him.

Opening the door to the staircase, he ascended the steep stairs, gripping the walls with his hands because there wasn't a railing. But he almost slipped from something wet on the wall. It smelled funny, like it had been washed with ammonia.

He turned onto the landing and flashed his light quickly but still saw no one.

He called out Dilipuncle's name.

He received no response.

Amrat's door was shut. Across from it was another room, what he assumed had been Priya's. The door was open, and a light breeze gushed through a window in the distance. He knocked on Amrat's door.

"Amrat!" he called.

No response.

He checked the knob, felt it was lukewarm, and turned it. He pushed the door open and quickly flashed the light around.

Another empty room. He was about to leave when he noticed the closet door was closed.

He approached it, slowly, and lit up the slit that passed for a knob.

"Amrat!" he called, but again, received no response.

He looked through the slit and thought he saw an eyeball stare back at him.

He put his fingers on the slit and yanked it open. He jumped back at the sight.

87

Amrat sat butterfly-style, his eyes closed, a chandlo pasted on his forehead, but Niral could tell the red dot wasn't painted with the normal kum kum powder. Rather, it was painted in blood. It was also embedded with tiny seeds, and his head was shaven, his hair in piles on his shoulders.

In his lap lay his father, his eyes closed, a gaping hole in his chest, and inside it, a lit candle of ghee rested on his crushed heart. On the floor was Priya's urn and a pair of bloody scissors.

Amrat opened his eyes.

"Niral, you have come to arrest me."

"I don't have the power," Niral said softly, the words barely a whisper.

"You should. We need enforcers in this world. That's what I never understood until today."

"You torched Gigglies too? You killed Lauren?"

"The Dock too. Have I forgotten any place? I couldn't get everything. I couldn't finish Vishal. Lauren told me everything the afternoon we woke, after I had broken my vows the night before with the one woman I thought I loved, a woman who said she would give up her life of sin to join her parents."

"Then why?"

"It was too much. The extent of corruption. I realized the world needed a cleansing, as Shiva accomplished in the myths, as Parashurama and other avatars have done throughout history when society degenerates. I simply put her out of her misery. She would never have quit at her age. If she sold her body here, she would do it in Maine, and her pain and that of society would never be vanquished.

"So I did what I could—I eliminated the evil I could. But I am only one man, and I can do only so much. From the beginning, I was not equipped to be an avatar. Neither were you."

"Amrat, this was wrong," Niral said.

"Action in the service of dharma is never wrong, Niral. Didn't Krishna say that to Arjuna? I would announce my case to the world, Niral, but I am lost as a man without my family. Now, I must join my Priya. As will you."

With three fingers, he gently lifted the candle out of Dilipuncle's chest.

"Vishal is gone, Amrat," Niral shouted. "You don't have to—"

But Amrat touched the candle to the wall. In a second, it lit up, and the flame engulfed the closet, then traveled along the slits of the ceiling.

In an instant, the fire became an inferno, encompassing every wall in the room and the floor too. Backing up, Niral witnessed Amrat on fire, burning with stoic aplomb, his skull now visible underneath his skin. Then, Niral felt the flame on his legs too, and intense pain over his whole body.

He dropped his flashlight and ran out of the room. Dark, black smoke made it impossible to breathe, so he crouched down. He could barely see, so he made a split-second decision to charge forward, galloping as fast as he could, until his legs hit something hard.

He bounced over the obstacle and landed on the sloping roof. He tumbled down, bouncing against the metal tiles until the wet sludge in the rain gutter blocked his trajectory and vanquished the flame. Dirt and the remnants of leaves covered his face and entered his mouth. He spat out some dirt and took one last look at the smoke before he closed his eyes, and darkness engulfed him.

PART VII

When Niral woke, he found himself in a hospital bed. Only able to see out of one eye, he saw he was covered with white bandages, his mother at his side, holding his hand.

"Niral, you are awake," she said. "We thought we would lose you."

She kissed his palm and placed her hand over his forehead like she did when he was a child, home from school with an illness.

She kept asking him how he felt, and he tried to tell her it would be fine, but he couldn't get anything out.

Then his father entered with Detective Sanchez and Detective Savard. Detective Sanchez began asking him something, but Niral went blank.

As Niral opened his right eye, he saw Detective Savard next to him, holding a pad. No one else was there.

"Niral, how do you feel?"

"Drowsy." Then, he felt the pain flow through his body.

He yelled. Detective Savard pushed the call button attached to the bed.

An hour later, after a nurse had increased his pain meds and knocked him out, Niral woke up. The doctor had arrived and was checking his bandages. "You've got second degree, partial thickness burns across half your body, Niral. The burns on the other half of your body are superficial. We thought maybe we might have to amputate your legs, but they seem okay now. You probably will be weak, so you'll need some prolonged exercise and therapy to regain strength. We had to do significant skin grafting on your legs as well as some on your torso and back. You've got scarring most places except your face, which mostly had first degree burns. But a couple of patches are there too. And you have a bandage over your left eye until it heals."

"Why did I feel so much pain?"

"That will come and go. We're pumping you full of morphine, which will dampen the pain, but it will come and go, especially with bandage changes and therapy. If it does increase too much, just let someone know, and the nurse will increase the dosage."

"I shouldn't have gotten involved," Niral said. "I should have left it alone like my father told me to."

Detective Savard responded, "You probably should have let us handle it, but you did what you could, Niral."

The doctor said, "Detective, he should be conscious enough now for you to ask a few questions," then left.

"I should have just died in the fire," Niral said.

"I'm glad you didn't," Detective Savard replied. "You're a good man, Niral. But there are some things you might want to know."

"What?" Niral asked, annoyed.

"Bob Macaday came to us. Told us about Coleman Investments, Vishal Patel's dealings, this guy Tragliani from the Lucchese. Everything."

"So you know."

"And your dad filled me in about Dilip Mehta. With the house burning, it's difficult to trace his DNA to the scarf, but the confession and his death should be good enough. Seems like the case is closed. Except for one thing: Vishal Patel is missing, and Tragliani's dead."

"Tragliani's dead?"

"He was assassinated the same day as the fires. Was sitting in his dining room in Maspeth, having dinner with his daughter, and someone shot him through the window. His bodyguards tailed the guy and gunned him down in the street. The shooter was Juan Garcia, identified by Bob Macaday as Vishal's chauffeur and personal bodyguard."

"So the Lucchese will take revenge. It'll never end."

"It's not clear. Who will they take revenge on? LedaCorp's holdings have been dissolved, all the money's missing, including the investment in Coleman and a bunch more with it. Seems like Vishal absconded, maybe left the country. The SEC told us they've suspected for a couple of years that he's had accounts in the Caymans."

"That's impossible. I..."

"What?"

"Nothing."

"Coleman is finished, most of the money is gone, and the feds will be seizing the rest during their investigations of money laundering, racketeering, land fraud, and bribes to public officials. A bunch of Lucchese have been arrested. And while we have evidence that Amrat committed all the arsons, the insurance companies don't have to pay a cent because they say Amrat Mehta acted on Vishal Patel's orders."

"That's insane."

"I guess we'll never know."

"It's not true. It's more complicated."

Detective Savard cleared his throat.

"I'm going to ask you to take that to your grave, Niral. Sanchez and I both agree that it's easier if we write it up as an arson for hire."

"That's wrong. Amrat never got any money."

"Look, Niral, you want Vishal or the Lucchese to argue that they should get the insurance money one day? It's possible. Anything's possible."

Niral breathed deeply.

"I just want to sleep."

His mother was by him when he woke again. So was an attractive Hispanic nurse, Gloria, who told Niral that it was time for his bath.

She removed the needles and tubes. They both helped him to the bathroom. In the mirror he saw his face, blotted with splotches of clear white skin, and the crisscrossed patch over his left eye.

Then the bandages came off, painfully, and Niral saw his wholly scarred body and his limp penis. The pain surged up into his legs and his torso, almost like some force was trying to break out of his bones. His body began contracting violently. The nurse ran back to the bed to give him another shot of morphine, while his mother hugged him for dear life and cried.

A few months later, he was discharged. As his father went to get the car, two familiar figures stood nearby. He asked his mother to get him a bottle of water, and as she went back into the hospital, Ricky and Wan approached.

"Hey, it's Captain Hook!" Ricky said, putting his arm around Niral.

"Remember, Niral, you owe us," Wan added. "We've got an assignment for you in Thailand. We've got operations there."

"What do you mean? I'm going home."

"You work for us now," Wan said, handing Niral some documents. "We've got your ticket, your visa, everything."

"Mad ladies for you there, too," Ricky added.

"Not like you got anything else going on, right?" Wan said, pushing the outline of a gun through his jacket.

Niral swallowed. "I guess not. My girl never came to see me. But what do I tell my parents?"

"That you're going there to teach English, Niral. You're a smart guy, right?"

In his basement apartment, now filled with pictures of Bhen and Bhai, Niral packed a duffel bag, stuffing it with underwear and a few clothes, which he figured was all he needed.

His father descended the stairs to the basement, holding a portrait of Bhen. His mother wept near the door.

"Take this with you, Niral," his father said. Your mother does not understand why you are going, but I know you want to spread Bhen's message."

"I forgot Bhen's message, Deddy."

Niral's father paused, forlorn. "Take the portrait. You will be reminded on the plane."

Niral stuffed it in his bag.

He prayed at his mother's feet. She pasted a chandlo onto his forehead. He closed his eyes. It felt cold.

At the airport, after his father had stopped the car, he came around and grabbed Niral's arm. "Remember Bhen, Niral. At least in your heart."

Niral held in tears. He placed his palms together. His father engulfed them in his own hands, squeezing tight. They touched foreheads. Finally, Niral turned and approached the revolving doors.

Once inside, he ripped open his duffel bag and threw Bhen's picture in the trash.

GLOSSARY OF TERMS

Arjuna—third of five Pandava brothers in the epic *Mahabharata*. He is an expert archer. During the war at Kurukshetra, he refuses to fight his relatives but receives an inspirational speech from his cousin Krishna (recorded in the *Bhagavad Gita*) and it changes his mind.

Atman (a. k. a. Brahman)—God, the divine life force. The combination of the three main Gods (or the Trimurti): Brahma (The Generator), Vishnu (The Operator), and Shiva (The Destroyer). Atman can be obtained through enlightenment in successive reincarnations, though beliefs vary.

Auntie—a respectful Anglo-Indian term for an elder woman.

Avatar—the form a God, usually Vishnu, takes when he or she incarnates on earth. This being, including humans like Krishna and animals like Matsya, a fish, profoundly alters world events. Most Hindus count ten avatars for Vishnu, but these beliefs vary. Some Hindus believe that Moses, Jesus, and Muhammad, among others, were also avatars.

Ayodhya—city in India where the epic *Ramayana* is based.

Bhagvan—Gujarati word for God (Atman).

Bhagavad Gita—the text of the dialogue of Arjuna—the third of the Pandava brothers—and his cousin Krishna had on the battlefield of Kurukshetra in the epic *Mahabharata*. It is considered one of the holiest texts in Hinduism.

Bhai—respectful term for brother.

Bhajan—holy Hindu songs, usually sung by groups of worshippers.

Bharat Natyam—a type of Indian dance performed by one dancer.

Bhen (also spelled "Ben")—respectful term for sister.

Bollywood—the large, contemporary Indian film industry.

Brahma—one of the three major Gods in Hinduism, known as the "Generator" because he is thought to have created the world.

Brahmin—one of the four major castes in Hinduism. Brahmins are the priests and scholars. If ranked hierarchically, they are the highest caste in terms of status and respect, though ideally, they are supposed to have little material wealth or power.

Chandlo—a red dot smudge on a forehead using kum kum powder. Usually applied when worshipping God in the temple or at home. Signifies, among other things, the worship of intelligence.

Chaniya Choli—a colorful, ornately embroidered and mirrored dress for women featuring a short top and skirt, including a decorative scarf called an odhni.

Deddy—short or affectionate Gujarati term for Father.

Dal—a soup made from split peas and lentils.

Dharma—one's righteous duty, or the right way. Contrasts with adharma, which is the wrong way or immorality.

Dhoti—a cloth that is wrapped around the groin and thighs.

Dikra—dear child.

Divo—a hand-created candle made of ghee.

Ghee—clarified butter.

Gujarati—people from the Northwestern state of Gujarat in India, and the language they speak.

Guru—sage or teacher.

Guru dakshina—in ancient India, a gift given to a teacher after a period of service.

Hiranyakashipu—corrupt king who received divine powers by praying to Brahma. He was not able to be killed during day or night, by man or beast, in earth or space, inside or outside, by animate or inanimate objects. Seeing Vishnu as his enemy, he became upset by his son Prahlad's unswerving devotion to Vishnu. After various methods of killing Prahlad failed, Vishnu incarnated himself as Narasimha, a half-man half-lion, and killed Hiranyakashipu with his claws at twilight in the middle of a doorway on his lap.

Holi—a spring festival inspired by Prahlad's triumph over Holika. Participants usually throw colors at each other and dance around a huge bonfire.

Holika—Hiranyakashipu's sister, who had the gift of not being burned by fire. Hiranyakashipu had her sit on a lit pyre with his son, Prahlad, on her lap, hoping to burn him to death, but when Prahlad prayed to Lord Vishnu, Holika died and Prahlad survived. It is the mythological inspiration for the Hindu holiday/spring festival Holi.

Janoi—a simple, multi-threaded string that is worn across the chest, over the left shoulder and under the right arm. It is received by Brahmin and Kshatriya boys after a Janoi ceremony, usually when they are teenagers. It represents their passage into their rightful role in society and their knowledge of prayers expected of their caste. Today, it is often merely given as a symbolic passage into manhood.

Kafni-pajama—a male dress featuring loose pajama bottoms and a long pullover shirt.

Kaka—respectful Gujarati term for blood uncle, though sometimes it is used for respected non-relatives in place of "Uncle."

Karma—a complex Hindu concept regarding one's actions and their cause and effect relationship to one's fate and reincarnation.

Khaman—a Gujarati snack made from gram flour.

Kohl—a black powder used as eye-makeup by Indians.

Krishna—one of the incarnations of Vishnu and a major character in the epic *Mahabharata*. A cousin of the Pandavas, he recites the *Bhagavad Gita* to Arjuna and serves as his charioteer during the battle of Kurukshetra.

Kshatriya—one of the four major castes in Hinduism. Kshatriyas are the warrior and kingly caste. If ranked hierarchically, they are considered the second highest caste after Brahmins.

Kum kum powder—a red powder used by Hindus for chandlos and other religious markings.

Kurukshetra—battlefield where the major battle in the *Mahabharata* occurs.

Laxmi—the Goddess of wealth and prosperity.

Mahabharata—the longest epic written in human history, authored by Veda Vyasa, who is also a minor character in it. Scholars differ on when it was written, but it was probably passed down orally by generations for thousands of years. The epic concerns the fate of the Kuru dynasty, from King Bharat to the death of Krishna. It features the *Bhagavad Gita* and the Kurukshetra war.

Mandir—a Hindu temple. In this case, a miniature version filled with small statues/pictures of Gods and candles.

Mata—respective term for mother or female Goddess in Gujarati.

Moksha—in Hinduism, liberation, perfection of consciousness, or becoming one with God. Can be obtained by human beings through four different methods: Jnana-Yoga (knowledge), Bhakti-Yoga (love, devotion), Raja-Yoga (meditation), and Karma-Yoga (action).

Mummy—short or affectionate term for Mother used by Gujarati people.

Odhni—a scarf worn with many Indian dresses, including a chaniya choli, sari, and punjabi.

Om—an Indian holy symbol, meaning, among other things, God.

Palathi—sitting position with legs crossed and feet either sticking out or under the thighs (butterfly-style).

Pandavas—five brothers who are primary characters in the *Mahabharata*.

Pandu—a character in the *Mahabharata*, descendent of the Kuru dynasty and father of Arjuna and the Pandavas.

Pappa—short or affectionate Gujarati term for Father.

Parashurama—the sixth avatar of Vishnu, considered to be the first warrior saint.

Patra—an Indian dish made of crushed chickpeas wrapped in big leaves from the Taro plant.

Perfect Man—a person who has reached moksha after successive births, and whose soul is thus ready to rejoin Atman upon death. This person sees the universe as God's lila, or playground, and is mentally detached from all things.

Prahlad—son of Hiranyakashipu and a devotee of Vishnu. His father tries to have him killed, but he survives due to his devotion.

Rakshasa—in Hindu mythology, a demon.

Rotli—a thin, round, flat, unleavened bread made of flour that is rolled, then heated.

Sanskrit—ancient Indian written language. Many of the ancient prayers are in this language.

Sanyasi—one who renounces worldly desires and concentrates on a spiritual life of detachment.

Sari—a traditional Indian dress for women consisting of a single cloth wrapped around the body, a petticoat, or lehenga, and a blouse, or choli.

Shak—the main staple of Gujarati meals. It consists of single or multiple vegetables cooked in oil. It is usually eaten with a rotli or other type of bread.

Shiva—one of the three major Gods in Hinduism. Known as the "Destroyer" because he has the power to destroy the world when it has become too corrupt.

Sudra—one of the four major castes in Hinduism. Sudras are the labor caste. If ranked hierarchically, they are the lowest caste, but theoretically carry the least responsibility.

Thali—a round dish usually made of steel, with many pockets for different types of Gujarati food.

Uncle—a respectful term for an adult male.

Vaishya—one of the four major castes in Hinduism. Vaishyas are the tradesmen, artisans, and merchants of society. If ranked hierarchically, they are the third highest caste.

Vedic—related to the teachings and traditions stemming from the *Vedas*, the ancient Hindu texts written in Sanskrit that are often cited as the oldest scriptures of Hinduism.

Vishnu—one of the three major Gods in Hinduism. Known as the "Operator" because he keeps the world running and steps in through incarnation when things are not going right.

Yoga—physical exercises from ancient Hindu scriptures.

STUDY GUIDE

1. Many of the characters in *The Brotherhood* have nicknames, sometimes multiple ones. What is the madam's nickname for Lance, and what is Lance's nickname for himself?

a) "The Asshole" and "PI"
b) "Iceman" and "CEO"
c) "Gigilo" and "CFO"
d) "Swordfish" and "The Manager"

2. What is the name of the company that owns real estate in Long Island City?

a) Devi Incorporated
b) The Brotherhood
c) Ledacorp
d) Coleman Investments

3. What neighborhood does Bob Macaday live in?

a) Ridgewood
b) Corona
c) Forest Hills
d) St. Albans

4. Lauren has complex relationships with most of the male characters in the novel. With which male character below does she have no known relationship?

a) Roberto Tragliani
b) Lance Portman
c) Justin
d) Martin

5. After Amrat teaches Lauren the Vedic ways, what is the gift she wants to give him called?

a) Guru Dakshina
b) Guru Vasanava
c) Guru Nirvana
d) Geisha Devya

6. Which business school does Priya Mehta attend?

a) Wharton School
b) Stern School of Business
c) Kellogg School of Management
d) McCombs School of Business

7. What is the theme of Jody Chou's bed cover?

a) Diary of a Wimpy Kid
b) Garfield
c) Calvin and Hobbes
d) Winnie the Pooh

8. Where does Niral find a bloody odhni?

a) Washington Square Park
b) Kissena Park
c) Flushing Meadow Park
d) Union Square

9. What is the name of the bread Niral's mother makes in Chapter 24?

a) Rotli
b) Bhakri
c) Pita
d) Roti

10. What is the name of the road Niral and Lauren cross to get to the boat headed to The Dock?

a) West Side Highway

b) FDR Drive
c) Grand Central Parkway
d) Belt Parkway

TRIVIA QUESTIONS

(YOU MAY NEED TO DO SOME RESEARCH OUTSIDE OF THE BOOK TO ANSWER THESE QUESTIONS!)

1. What is the literary inspiration for the title/organization The Brotherhood?

2. Which university was Tejas Desai attending when he wrote the first incarnation of *The Brotherhood*?

3. Who are Tejas Desai's three favorite classic authors?

4. Which noir author does Tejas Desai admire who often sets his books in Detroit?

5. Which publication named Queens the best destination on earth in 2015?

6. What year was The New Wei founded?

7. Where did Tejas Desai acquire his MFA in Creative Writing?

ANSWERS TO STUDY GUIDE AND TRIVIA QUESTIONS

Answers:

Study Guide

1) b
2) d
3) c
4) c
5) a
6) b
7) d
8) d
9) a
10) b

Trivia Questions

1) *Invisible Man* by Ralph Ellison
2) Wesleyan University
3) Balzac, Faulkner and Dostoyevsky
4) Elmore Leonard
5) Lonely Planet
6) 2012
7) Queens College

ACKNOWLEDGMENTS

I must thank many people for helping with this reissue of *The Brotherhood*. First and foremost, my parents, who somehow continue to be supportive, occasionally, of my writing endeavors despite my very slowly building success. Kacper Jarecki and Matthew Allison helped me film the fundraising video for the GoFundMe campaign that financed publication of this book. Kacper assisted in editing the video, too, and Matthew served as a valuable beta reader and cheerleader for the series. Vijay R. Nathan had me on his Radio Free Brooklyn radio show, *Truth to Power*. Other beta readers for The Brotherhood Chronicle included Robert Ballard, Panth Naik, and Anasuya Desai.

My wonderful cover designer Fena Lee, who works tirelessly on my behalf despite her busy medical school schedule. Copyeditor Christine Keleny, both meticulous and determined, has copyedited the manuscript fearlessly and even given developmental critiques. Ashley Evans proofread this book to perfection.

Gary Scudero had me on his Queens Public Television show, *Talents Unlimited*, and many radio show hosts have done the same in the past. My many friends and acquaintances across the world, on social media and in real life, have supported and engaged me. I want to thank, especially, the many donors, public and anonymous, who have funded this publication through GoFundMe. This has included extended family, old friends, new acquaintances, and complete strangers. Without your support, this reissue might not have been possible, and I am greatly appreciative.

Finally, the borough of Queens in New York City: for most of my life, you've given me a home, a perch, and a laboratory for my work. At times, you've frustrated me, and I've frustrated you, but you've never given up on me, and I don't plan to give up on you.

Tejas Desai
September 2018

COMING SOON...

THE BROTHERHOOD CHRONICLE

VOLUME TWO: *THE RUN AND HIDE*

BOOK ONE, PART I, CHAPTER 6 & 7

SETTING: BANGKOK, THAILAND

Niral sped through the heart of Bangkok and toward Sukhumvit. He parked his motorcycle next to the Skytrain stairs. A boy with no legs sat by it, holding out a cup.

Niral ignored him. Angrily, he stared at two Indians who flirted with a ladyboy outside a bar next to the staircase he took up to Same Same. The walls of the staircase were graffitied with funny statements and drawings of sex acts.

Once upstairs, he passed through door beads into a well-lit waiting area with a bar tended, as usual, by a Dragon henchman named Mok.

"Niral! Welcome!" he exclaimed. Then he noticed the head. "You finished the job?"

"How do you know?"

"We gossip. You know us."

"I heard Mr. Hong is in town. Is he here?"

"Duncan sent you?" Mok asked, laughing. "I know you would not come on your own. Let me tell Nam you are here."

He walked through a lavish blue curtain. Niral waited for a few minutes. He regarded the head as his hands continued to shake but for a different reason than before. Mok re-emerged from the curtain, followed by a

232

shorter, wiry fellow with a long Dragon tattoo down both his arms.

Nam slapped Niral on the back. "Long time, Khun Niral. You brought a present. Mr. Hong will be happy. Come."

Niral was shocked by Nam's congeniality. He followed his former harasser through the dark tunnel of the club toward a table where Mr. Hong sat, drinking some Johnnie Walker Red Label in a shot glass. Mr. Hong smiled at Niral, who tried to wai to him with his hands full. Mr. Hong stood tall and handsome in his beige suit and took the head.

He removed the cloth and stared at Thanat's face.

Mr. Hong nodded at Niral.

"Good. Sit."

Niral did as ordered. Mr. Hong turned the head so it faced Niral. The shocked expression that still lasted past Thanat's final breath made Niral shudder.

Nam pulled up a chair and placed two more shot glasses on the table. He took the bottle of Johnnie Walker and began to pour, but Mr. Hong put his hand over the glass.

"Let the youngest pour," Mr. Hong said, "the poo noy."

Nam appeared angry, but he deferred to his boss. He performed his wai to Mr. Hong as earnestly as possible, holding his hands high above his head. Niral's hands were still shaking as he took the bottle and spilled some whiskey over Nam's glass and onto Nam's pants.

Nam glared at Niral sharply, but Mr. Hong laughed, diffusing the situation as Thais did. Nam had no choice but to practice the custom of "cool heart" and imitate his laugh.

"I'm sorry," Niral said nevertheless, out of force of habit.

"You've proven yourself a Dragon," Nam forced himself to say. "We

233

should tattoo your back."

"He is scarred already," Mr. Hong said, laughing. "He has done well. He is not a Dragon yet, but he can become one."

"True, we can't have a gay Dragon," Nam reminded him.

"We will cure him yet," Mr. Hong said. He raised his glass. "To honor and respect. To saving face from sia naa."

They drank. Niral felt the sting down his throat and coughed.

"I love Thailand. Do you love Thailand?" Mr. Hong asked Niral.

Niral nodded.

"It is Candyland," Mr. Hong continued. "It is my home. I go to Hong Kong, Singapore, Shanghai, Seoul. The Chinese there try to tell me I am home, but my home is Thailand. This place is sanuk, all the time." He held his glass up. "I am glad Duncan took you. You have grown. But you are still too dark in the mind. Come to Scandal tonight. You, Duncan, Rob. Apsara will be there too. We will celebrate our victory over evil with sanuk mai krap."

"I don't know..." Niral began to say.

"Don't worry, man," Nam interrupted, slapping Niral on the back. "We'll have some ladyboys for you."

"Or some boys," Mr. Hong said, laughing.

Niral's phone buzzed, and he sighed. He saw a text from Rob.

"I have to go, Mr. Hong," he said. "I have a pickup to make."

"Of what?"

"Diamonds. From our supplier."

"Make sure it is not glass," Mr. Hong said.

"We do every time."

"The time you didn't wasn't good," Nam reminded him.

Niral got up. "I hope we won't have to do this again."

"Me too," Mr. Hong replied, rising too. "I don't want a war with Sumantapat. He must not find out."

"He won't. Rob cleaned up the mess."

"Good."

Niral made a deep wai to him, and Mr. Hong nodded back. Nam acknowledged him warily.

"See you tonight," Mr. Hong said.

7

Niral sped back across Bangkok, past colorful wats, swarming European tourists, and a Hindu ceremony for Ganesh, breathing in the gasoline exhaust as he snaked through Silom, down Charoen Krung Road, then south along the Chao Phraya river.

He passed through a hole in a chain-linked fence and stopped near a warehouse on the shore. Rob's motorcycle was parked outside. Inside, he was at the table, magnifier in his eye, examining a diamond he had just unwrapped.

Shekhat, the merchant, was standing near the doorway. His brothers were eating some rotli-shak dal-bath at the far end of the warehouse.

"Niralbhai," Shekhat said in Gujarati, "you are late."

"I was on the other side of Bangkok."

"Your partner is good. Watch out for your job."

"Are you raising the price again?" he asked, ignoring Shekhat's comment.

"You must understand, my shipment costs are increasing. Even under

Modi, the government is not good. Taxes, regulation. I have been giving Duncan a break. But I have no choice now."

"You've already raised the price twice. You will force us to find another merchant. Or buy it online. Or go to the source."

"The source?" Shekhat laughed. "You will fly to India to buy it there? You know online has shipping costs too. Understand, I am a reasonable businessman."

"We'll do what it takes. We've been loyal customers. We don't need to give an excuse."

Shekhat's face turned grim. "Niralbhai, I have asked around about you to my family in Surat. They have contacts in Yam Gam. You were a Brotherhood follower."

Shekhat had tried to befriend Niral through their mutual Gujarati background, but he had never before brought up The Brotherhood or Niral's past.

"I was a Brotherhood follower, that's true," Niral replied. "What business is it of yours?"

"You must understand, while I was not a Brotherhood member, I loved Bhen. I know Bhai has been different, but I did love Bhen when she was alive. And following her teachings, I try to be fair in my business. So if I did not have to raise prices, I would not. But I will tell you this: because you are a brother, if you want to go into business with me, independent of Duncan, I am willing to listen."

Niral shook his head. "I think I'll go help Rob," he said.

Niral took out his magnifier and went to work, unwrapping each diamond and making sure the specifications were met regarding clarity, cut, weight, and color. Even one scratch would result in rejection. They separated the stones that were damaged or didn't seem to match the dimensions. Then, of the ones they selected, they determined which were worth purchasing based on the price. Finally, they matched each stone against a list Duncan had emailed them.

"You'll take off 20 percent for the batch like usual, mate?" Rob asked. "We'll take more then."

"This time, I can take off 15 percent," Shekhat replied.

"That's highway robbery, mate."

"Call it what you want. You can decide."

Rob smirked. He took out wads of baht and slapped them on the table. Then he slipped the diamonds, rewrapped now, into the bag.

"You won't believe what I had in this bag before," Rob said. "Don't guess."

"Your friend is strange," Shekhat said to Niral in Gujarati. "But he is smart."

Niral figured this jab was due to his rejection of Shekhat's suggestion. He wasn't sure what either of them would gain out of collaborating: it was probably just a business tactic used to gain favor. He hadn't heard The Brotherhood mentioned in years, and he doubted Shekhat had ever followed Bhen.

CPSIA information can be obtained
at www.ICGtesting.com
Printed in the USA
FSHW021749181120
76078FS